AN AVALON ROMANCE

COUNTRY CHARMED
Nicola Merrells

Taryn Christiansen never shied away from hard work, yet the challenges she was facing were growing too quickly. She'd landed at the remote Aspen Creek Inn and Ranch desperate to prove herself as a hotel manager. If she could turn a profitable season for the troubled inn, a dream job at a glamorous downtown hotel was within her grasp.

She didn't expect to fall in love with her co-manager, the disarmingly intuitive cowboy, Douglas Prescott. Or count on the small Aspen Creek community instilling a warm sense of home and belonging to her battered heart. She suddenly had every reason to stay.

However, the very reasons she left her former job to find peace and solace are returning. The news of her previous employer's involvement in the inn's imminent foreclosure takes her by surprise and adds to her dismay. To make matters even more complicated, her ex-boyfriend, also a former co-worker, has launched a blackmail and slander campaign against her.

Taryn had gained everything at Aspen Creek, and now risks losing it all.

COUNTRY CHARMED

•

Nicola Merrells

AVALON BOOKS
NEW YORK

PRINTED IN THE UNITED STATES OF AMERICA
ON ACID-FREE PAPER
BY HADDON CRAFTSMEN, BLOOMSBURG, PENNSYLVANIA

Great friends don't need to prove themselves, but some find ways to do so anyway. A special thank you to Lisa K. Mason and Heidi Sheard for reading, re-reading, proofing, editing, and endless encouragement.

Great husbands, of course, simply have it in their nature to prove themselves every single day. So another special thank you to Mark, for helping me make time to write and for being ever-willing to explore and enjoy story settings with me, no matter how distant.

And finally to our friends at the historic Quilchena Hotel and Ranch, the magical place on which the setting for Aspen Creek is based, a big thank you for sharing your world and always making our family feel at home.

Chapter One

Taryn jumped in her seat as fingers of lightning exploded across the sky. Hitting the brakes in a reflex action, she sent her car into a skid on the narrow gravel road. A deafening clap of thunder pushed her heart further into her throat. Desperately, she cranked the steering wheel hard to the left as her front wheel slid into the ditch, the grating sound filling her with dread.

Wide-eyed, heart thumping wildly, she killed the motor and scrambled out of the car. Thunder began to rumble through the valley in earnest. "No-o-o-o!" she shouted into the storm. Her car's undercarriage lay grounded on the soft shoulder, the wheels embedded in the ditch. "Not this! Not now! Not after everything else!" She kicked a tire in frustration.

The tempest burst into the valley with full force. Fierce winds drove trees and shrubs into submission; branches bowed and swayed while leaves swirled through the air. Hunching her shoulders, Taryn crossed her hands over her chest in a timeless protective gesture, disbelief turning into despair.

Then the sky opened and it began to pour.

So much for the short cut suggested by the woman at the service station. "I can't believe this is happening," Taryn muttered to herself as she rubbed her temples. The drive from Vancouver to the mountainous interior of British Columbia had taken longer than she had expected. Now she was stuck here with no idea if anyone ever traveled this pot-holed excuse for a road. She sighed, long and loud. New job, first meeting, and she was going to be late. Lovely.

Suddenly a bobbing light across the valley caught her eye. Taryn sat up, squinting through the rain-streaked glass, then rolled down the window to get a better view, trying to ignore the rain pelting her face.

Two lights. Headlights. They appeared and disappeared without rhythm, likely blocked by trees as the vehicle made its way down the distant hillside.

Rolling up the window, she continued to watch, willing the lights to come her way, but the trees blocked her view when the vehicle reached the valley bottom. She held her breath as her eyes desperately searched for another glimpse of what seemed to be her vestige of hope.

Suddenly the headlights appeared again, bouncing along the road just below her. As they neared, she could see they belonged to a dark blue pickup truck, driven by—Taryn hit the wiper button again and peered through her windshield for a better look—someone with a large frame wearing a cowboy hat. A man. Her heart sank and a quiver of fear shot through her. This situation would have felt safer if her assistance had come from a woman, she thought.

The truck pulled up, stopping just a few feet away from her car. Smiling weakly, she rolled down her window, eyeing the man as he rolled down his own.

He rested a solid, denim-clad arm on the window's edge and leaned out slightly. "Need some help?" The sound of his deep, smooth voice offered a complete contrast to the howling of the wind and rain.

Her stomach flipped, just once, as she stared at him, a small smile stuck on her face. A rugged male cowboy model from a fashion advertisement was her first thought—perfect marketing material. A strong jaw line sported the beginning of a five o'clock shadow and framed a hard mouth with lips that turned up slightly at the edges in the hint of a grin. The cowboy's black hair was fairly short, just long enough at the back to curl a bit as it brushed the collar of his denim jacket. His face and the hand resting on the window's edge were slightly tanned, not the holiday-on-the-beach type of tan, but the kind of burnished bronze that comes from working outside in all kinds of weather.

Taryn watched the stranger's eyes, the same color as the leaden sky above, as they moved over her vehicle, perhaps in an attempt to assess the damage. They then settled on her face, which was still being battered with rain through the open window. Yes, she thought, momentarily captivated, they were definitely the color of storm clouds, though without the turbulence. And they were locked onto hers, turning her mind to mush. She swallowed and cleared her throat slightly.

"I'm stuck," she said finally.

"I gathered that." Turning slightly, he brought his other arm onto the window's edge, his broad shoulders filling the opening. He rested his chin on his forearms as if settling down to wait.

Don't let him unbalance you, Taryn. You're in a bit of a mess right now. Taking a restorative breath, she said, "My front wheel's lodged in the ditch. I can't get out. I—umm— have to get to the Aspen Creek Inn this afternoon. The woman at the service station suggested this route when I asked her how I could make better time. I wanted to beat the storm."

"Looks like you didn't." He smiled.

Ah, funny man, she thought sarcastically. "Do you think you could get me out?"

Without lifting his head from its resting place on his forearms, he moved his gaze back and forth along the car. "Not today, I don't think."

"What?" Indignant, she suddenly had no trouble looking into his handsome face. "What do you mean, *not today?* You're not going to help? Whatever happened to country hospitality? Aren't there any tow trucks around?"

She caught the glint in his eyes. His apparent amusement at her irritation did nothing for her mood.

"I can help you, but I can't get you out." He leaned back into his seat and gestured with his head. "Hop in and I'll give you a ride to the inn. How's that for country hospitality?"

"But what about my car?"

"When we get to the inn you can call a tow truck. There's only one around here, and he's gone into town today. He can give you a tow tomorrow," he said simply, as if all her problems were solved.

She watched him for a moment, indecisive, her mind churning. Overall, he seemed tough, but not unkind; powerful, yet patient. Taryn sensed in him a benevolence that made her initial fears about encountering a male stranger on this isolated road subside somewhat. But there were other worries.

"I can't leave all my stuff." Losing her possessions was a concern, and so was what sitting in his truck cab with him would do to her heart rate. She must be overly sensitive because of all the stress in her life recently, she told herself. Sure, in the past couple of months she'd been both assaulted and betrayed by her co-worker. There'd been her awkward rejection of his affections, the angry exchange that followed, then the resulting resignation from a job she loved. His recent angry phone call, threatening retribution for Taryn's warning a wealthy friend away from him, turned out to be the last thing Taryn's frayed nerves could handle. A nagging dread gnawed at her stomach at the memory. She swallowed hard, turning her mind back to the problem at hand. Still, she reasoned, in light of all that, facing this western male model-type shouldn't turn her into putty like this.

She was a professional, after all, and had completed a number of courses on how to communicate with all different kinds of people.

"Just take what you need for tonight. Look around you." Her gaze followed one of his sculptured hands as it made a sweeping gesture over the valley. "No one's going to steal anything."

"Maybe you could tow me," Taryn suggested, her expression brightening with the idea. "My transmission is shot, but the brakes work. Could you pull me out and tow me to the service station so I can get my car fixed?"

Cowboy Man shook his head. "Nothing to tow you with."

Her gaze moved past him to the rope hanging against the back window of his truck cab. "What about that rope?"

"It's not a rope, it's a lariat," he said without turning around. "It's for roping livestock."

"Couldn't you make an exception? I'm sure the livestock won't mind." Was he teasing her?

He raised an eyebrow sceptically, as if trying to gage whether she were joking, then shook his head slightly. "Tying the lariat to your bumper would ruin its shape, stretch it, put kinks in it, and," eyeing the luggage pressed against the back window of the car, he added, "judging by the amount of stuff you have packed in there, probably snap it clean through."

She paused. "I see." But she didn't see. Not really. A cowboy rule, perhaps. Since he was obviously her only way out of this mess, it was probably best not to press the point.

Taryn glanced at his face again, frustrated at the amusement and challenge she saw there. *He knows I don't want to get into that truck with him.* Tension tightened her neck and shoulders. Well, there was no way around it, she reasoned. If he meant to do her any harm—a notion that seemed increasingly unlikely as she continued to speak with him—he could just as easily do it here as in his truck. Even so, perhaps filling his truck cab with her belongings would provide some measure of symbolic protection.

She dropped her shoulders and sighed. "I'll just get a few of my things." Now resolved, she opened her car door and climbed out with some effort, finding that the front wheel being embedded in the ditch had tilted her car at an awkward angle. Cowboy Man, as she inwardly referred to him, had stopped his truck so close to her car that she had to side-step quickly to avoid brushing within inches of his face.

Taryn was suddenly self-conscious about her appearance. The rain had pasted her curls to her scalp and her damp blouse clung to her skin. She must look like a drowned rat, she thought. Hoping to restore some order, she ran her fingers through her hair and under her eyes, then wiped her face with the sleeve of her blouse, trying to ignore that he was watching her every move with ardent interest.

"No, thanks." She held up her hand to stop him as he moved to get out of his truck. "I can manage." The last thing she needed now was the sensory onslaught of his entire being beside hers helping unload the car. What she had seen through the window had unnerved her enough already. Besides, she was determined to show some independence through this unfortunate encounter.

Turning quickly, Taryn moved to the back of the car, warily eyeing the muddy water running in the ditch. It was about four inches deep. If she could straddle the ditch she'd be in a perfect position to get a few of her bags from the trunk. It was a stretch, but—she eyed the opposite bank— not impossible.

"If you're about to do what I think you are, I'd advise against it," the man said from his vantage point in the truck. "Here," he opened the door, "let me give you a hand."

"I can manage on my own, thanks" she insisted. Stepping gingerly, she reached her foot to the opposite bank and held it there for an instant before the muddy ground gave way.

Less than a minute later, having removed most of the mud from her clothes, Taryn sat in the front seat of the stranger's truck. The heat of total embarrassment burning her cheeks was slow to subside. The fact that he had not laughed outright when she had landed in the ditch, and the fact that he had not yet said those four most infuriating words—*I told you so*—were little consolation at the moment. He had been there in a flash, strong hands almost entirely encircling her waist, helping her up, then quickly and silently digging around in the truck for a towel. No laughter, but the merriment flashing in his eyes made her blood boil.

He handed her the towel. "I just want to say—"

"I'd really appreciate it if you didn't say anything," she said rather sharply. She eyed him warily, ready to deflect any quips.

He gave her a slow, deliberate smile. "I can see you're beating yourself up on the inside, and I was just going to tell you not to be so hard on yourself. If it's any consolation, you're beautiful when you're dirty; it's sort of a cute street-urchin appeal."

A winsome flirt, she concluded, and quickly looked away, trying to hide the flaring heat in her cheeks. She busied herself with the towel. *Nicely done, Taryn,* she thought, disgusted at her inability to come up with an appropriate retort.

He turned back to her car. "So, how about I give you a—"

"Yes. A hand with my bags would be very kind," she managed tightly, vigorously brushing off her jeans in a useless attempt to remove the mud stains.

"Which bag do you want me to pull out?" he asked.

Her heart sagged with defeat as she looked over at her car. Things were just not going right this week, this month, this year. This new job was supposed to turn things around. Now she was wet, dirty, embarrassed, stranded, *and* late. She was also dependent upon a cowboy whose soft gray eyes and easy smile made her head spin—and to whom she had proven she was a total dolt—to drive her to the inn. There was so little certainty in her life at the moment; the thought of abandoning her car and belongings in this wilderness only to arrive at a strange place where huge responsibilities would be placed on her shoulders suddenly became over-whelming. She swallowed hard, hoping to dislodge the lump that was forming in her throat.

"Could we bring everything?" Her voice caught slightly.

"Everything?" He sounded incredulous as he turned to look at her. Something in her face must have warned him off making a crack, and his expression softened. "It would all get wet and dirty in the back of the pickup. Why don't you just take what you need for overnight, and we can arrange to get the rest tomorrow?"

Her shoulders slumped. "My life is in that car," she said quietly, shifting her gaze from the car to his face. She didn't care anymore if he amused himself at her expense. The day couldn't get much worse.

One of the man's hands moved up to rest consolingly on Taryn's shoulder. It seemed such a friendly, gentle gesture that she didn't pull away. He smiled. "Your livelihood may be connected with that car and what's in it, but don't ever get your livelihood confused with your life. Your life is in here," he said, lifting his forefinger and gently touching her temple, "and in here;" he lowered his finger and barely touched the bone just under the hollow of her throat. He winked then, breaking the spell, and in one fluid motion, turned and went back to her car.

"If you don't tell me which one or two of these you want, I'll just pick any," he said, his long, strong legs straddling the ditch with ease.

Taryn stared after him, the places where he had touched her now tingled, and she wondered absently if they would still be tingling tomorrow. Shaking her head slightly to clear her mind, she took a deep breath, and felt that she had, somehow, been given a reprieve—the first one in many weeks.

"Well?" He was bending over her trunk, ready to grab a bag, and she noticed with a small, reluctant smile that he could indeed pass for one of those cowboy models—he certainly wore his denims well.

"The, uhh, dark blue duffel bag and . . . oh, my purse. And the keys out of the ignition."

They bumped along the gravel road in silence for a few minutes. Cowboy Man didn't take up more than his share of the cab's bench seat, but something about his presence filled the cab to capacity. It was more than the broad shoulders, the long muscled legs, and the sweep of his strong neck and jaw line, all reminding Taryn of a Greek statue. It was . . . well, his aura of total masculinity. There was no other word for it. And it was all the more striking because it brought out in her an acute awareness of her own femininity—mud and all. He even smelled good, she thought resentfully, trying not to inhale the intoxicating combination of rain-soaked forest and sandalwood emanating from him.

No ring on his finger; she gave herself a mental shake for noticing, then pulled her gaze away from the strong hand wrapped loosely around the steering wheel. What was wrong with her? She certainly didn't have the mental energy to waste on these frivolities, considering her current challenges and her recent disasters. She diverted her attention to the scene outside her window. The storm had moved on. She could see the flint-colored clouds in the distance, likely wreaking havoc over the next hill.

The valley brightened as the sunshine returned, bringing with it a muggy warmth. She rolled down her window, welcoming the breeze on her face. They were crossing the valley floor now, its flat surface a sea of tall green grass swaying slightly in the wind, like small waves on a lake. Hayfields. Fodder for livestock, she assumed, noticing a few cattle grazing on the rough scrub in the distance.

"So how did you happen to be driving on this road during

· a storm?" she asked, keeping her gaze on the landscape.

"Lucy from the service station called to say that she'd directed a 'city person in a little car' along the shortcut road to the inn. When the storm broke she was worried and called me to make sure you'd made it. I asked around. No one had seen you, so I came to check."

"Oh . . . I see." That was nice of him, she thought. And it was nice of that Lucy woman too. She wished she had not asked, though, as a little voice inside prompted her to re-member her manners and thank him. She'd rather avoid expressions of indebtedness in the close proximity of the truck cab. Plus then there was that little bit about his barely restrained mirth at her mishap. She stole a look at him and managed a quick, "Well, thank you."

"Don't mention it." He glanced at her and grinned. "It's been . . . interesting."

She set her jaw and stared out the window again. There went the Greek statue comparison; Taryn was certain they never grinned like that. *Insolent man.*

"There's an old miner's shack along this route. I'll stop there so you can change."

Thoughtful, she acknowledged reluctantly. "That would be fine, thanks," she said evenly, her gaze fixed on the land-scape to her right.

"Hang on!"

Lurching back in her seat as he hit the accelerator, Taryn looked ahead just in time to see the truck's front end drop into a swollen creek bed. With a yelp she grabbed the edge of her seat as the wheels hit the water, which was as deep as the tires were high. The truck ploughed through the current, sending a steady spray up the fenders and right through her open window, drenching the side of her head and her right shoulder—and most of the rest of her before she got the window closed.

The cowboy pulled to a stop on the other side of the creek,

then turned to look at her for a long moment, his mouth twitching as he fought back another smile. "Why was your window open?" he asked finally, as though having rolled it down were the strangest thing in the world.

Too shocked for words, Taryn could only stare at him with angry surprise, blinking rapidly as water dripped off her hair and down her face. This was unbelievable! Her chest rose and fell as she took deep breaths, barely controlling her temper.

"You . . . ! How could you? Wha—" she sputtered, trying to get the words out through clenched teeth. "You . . . You could have warned me!" She flung the door open and jumped out, uselessly brushing at her clothes. She glared at him, hands on her hips, legs apart, as though defending a piece of ground. Well, she was defending something. As soon as she found a shred of dignity, she would defend it to her dying breath.

He leaned over onto her vacated seat. "I didn't notice your window was open, really." He paused, then added, "Are you always this accident prone?" he said as his eyes met hers again.

"Impertinent lout."

Unfazed, he replied, "You may want to step over a bit."

She glanced down. With an exhale resembling a whimper she covered her face with her hands. It was beyond saving now; the humiliation was complete. Her left heel was buried in a pile of cow dung.

She cleaned her shoe—and the rest of herself as best she could—in the offending creek. After she climbed back into the truck they drove in silence for the next while. Taryn glared at him a number of times. He stared straight ahead, focused on the rough road, but she didn't miss the occasional twitching of his beautifully shaped mouth. She guessed he was recounting the events since meeting her, providing himself with considerable amusement. She mentally reviewed them too, concluding that Cowboy Man was bad luck—handsome as sin, but bad luck. The sooner she could get to the inn and away from him, the better.

The road took them out of the valley, up onto the next rise, and into a more heavily forested area. Cowboy Man slowed the truck as they neared an old shack. "This is it. I'll wait here," he said, pulling off the road to stop beside the door.

Taryn looked at the derelict old hovel with some scepticism, wondering if the inside was as unwelcoming as the outside, but said nothing and headed for the door. *Any port in a storm,* she reminded herself as she gingerly pushed the door open and peered inside. *And this one's good enough.*

The dimness of the shack's interior stopped her for a moment. She let her eyes adjust before shutting the door with her foot. Arms full of clothes and toiletries, she looked around for somewhere to set down her things and begin her metamorphosis from street urchin, as Cowboy Man had so charmingly put it, to confident hotel manager.

The choices were limited. In one corner sat a dirty old wood stove that would probably fetch a thousand dollars in an urban antique shop. A stack of firewood supported one leaning wall. A small, glassless window was the shack's only source of light. Beneath it, a wooden table hosted two lopsided chairs. She headed toward the table and deposited her load on its dusty surface.

Within minutes, her hair was toweled almost dry and finger-combed into a semblance of order. Her face was clean again, with mascara and clear lipgloss quickly re-applied. She had just slipped on a clean pair of jeans and was struggling with the buttons of a fresh blouse when she noticed a shadow across the window.

She slowly raised her head. Her blue eyes locked with grey.

But they were not the grey eyes of a man.

Taryn screamed and jumped back, shock and fear turning her legs to jelly. The wolf began yelping, trying to pull itself into the shack through the tiny window. Unable to regain her balance, Taryn fell backwards against the door with a thud, her right hand blindly groping for the latch behind her, her heels skidding out from under her as she fought to right herself.

She felt the door opening against her back, heaved herself forward slightly to let it open, then lost her footing and fell against it again. "What the hell?" A man's voice rumbled as the door crashed open with enough force to propel her forward onto the floor boards, knocking the wind out of her.

The wolf was now on the table, barking wildly. Taryn scrambled to her feet as Cowboy Man rushed in. "Grab a weapon," she croaked as she struggled to inhale, grabbing his denim jacket for balance with her right hand while reaching for a piece of firewood.

"Get down!" he roared, and she quickly crouched on the floor, both hands now clutching the piece of wood in a death grip. Did he bring a gun? Was he about to shoot the animal?

"No! Not you!" He tried to pull Taryn up by her arm. "You!" he shouted. He pointed at the wolf, now quiet and staring at him with its tail wagging, and then pointed at the floor. "Get down and sit! Now!"

Weak-kneed and bewildered, Taryn looked at her rescuer and then at the wolf. The animal jumped down from the table to the chair, and then to the floor. Her heart pounded in her chest, her body trembled, and she was still unable to fully grasp what was going on. She felt like she was going to be sick.

"I said sit!" The wolf's rear end slowly sank to the floor and it stared at the two humans with its head cocked to one side.

"Are you alright?" She could hear the concern in his voice as he turned her toward him, examining her face and arms. She stared at him, speechless, her limbs like rubber. He gently lifted each of her trembling hands, noting the scrapes on their heels where she had hit the floor when he charged the door.

"I think I'm okay," she managed. The shock of the escapade was slow to subside. She felt hollow and nauseated.

"Are your hands okay to work the buttons, or do you want help?"

She glanced down at her blouse and noticed that the three bottom buttons remained undone. Silently, she fumbled her way through them, willing her hands to stop shaking, hating to have him see her so discomposed.

Smoothing her blouse, she forced her attention on the offending animal. "That's your wolf?"

"He's not a wolf. He's a Shepherd-Malamute cross. His name's Chip." He glared at the animal. "Wolves don't bark, incidentally," he added.

She digested that for a moment. "What the heck was he doing?" Her strength was returning, peppered with equal doses of indignation and exasperation.

"I left him at home today. Where you should have stayed, you wily beast." He pointed a finger at the beast in question, silently ordering him to remain seated. Chip's tail thumped in response. "But the storm, mostly the lightening, probably, spooked him. My cabin's about four miles down the dirt road that branches off behind this shack. We sometimes stop here for lunch in bad weather when I'm checking fences. I guess he was looking for me, saw the truck parked outside, and thought I was in here without him. He's not dangerous." He pointed at Chip again, who'd been about to rise, giving him a fierce look until the dog's rear end sunk down again. "You just need to be firm with him," he said matter-of-factly.

"Firm with him," she repeated flatly, sighing with resignation. "Tell you what. Why don't you be firm with him and get him out of here so I can collect my things. Wait—" she stopped his arm as he reached for Chip. "Look at your hand. You're bleeding."

He paused to examine his hand. "It's nothing. Caught in the door, I think, when you fell against it."

She shook her head. The gash was at least an inch long, and still bleeding slightly. "No, it's not nothing. It needs to be disinfected and wrapped. I had the worst infection once when I was a kid . . ." She bent her head to rummage through her toiletries and continued talking into her bag, "Just from a cardboard cut. Nearly went gangrenous. They almost had to amputate my finger. My mother jokingly said it was a sign, since the cardboard box held a gift from my father, and they'd just gone through a bitter divorce." Why was she babbling on like this? Post-traumatic stress? *Shut up, Taryn!* "I usually have some basic first aid stuff in here . . . Ah, this will do." She produced a tiny bottle of rubbing alcohol and looked up at him.

He was watching her with an odd expression on his face: half puzzled, half amused.

And why wouldn't he be, Taryn? What on earth are you going on about? Pull it together.

"Might sting like the dickens, though," she added quietly, wanting to reach for his injured hand, but suddenly afraid to move.

"What about your hands?" He asked, breaking their eye contact and stepping toward a small cupboard behind the wood stove. He brought out a first aid kit and flipped it open.

She looked at the heels of her hands again. Slight scrapes, skin barely broken. "Nothing a good wash won't clean." But she accepted the disinfectant towelette and ointment from him.

She made quick work of her own clean up, wincing as she watched him awkwardly attend to his own cut using his left hand. "Here, let me," she said.

"If you insist." He let her take his hand. "But I'm a little sceptical about having someone as calamitous as you doctoring me."

"How charming," she said with a sardonic smile, then added, "Don't you trust me?"

"Innately, it would seem. Which is strange, since we've just met," he said with a sudden frown, as if the realization both surprised and troubled him.

Her smile disappeared as well. He'd lost his bantering tone, and was searching her face intently. And then, with a quick "I'm drawing the line at stitches though," he turned his face toward Chip, commanding the slinking dog to sit down again—and the moment was gone.

Taryn bowed to clean the cut, trying not to let the curious exchange—the surprising heat and solidity of his hand in hers, and the nearness of his body—distract her from her work. Her fingers looked pale and small next to his, and she guessed he could probably entirely envelope her hand within his, had he a mind to do so.

Which he does not, of course, she told herself sternly. "Bandage?"

She covered the cut, the silence in the shack broken only by the cowboy command to Chip to leave with him. As she collected her things, Taryn tried to shake the oddly intense sensation of intimacy that seemed to settle on her shoulders like a warm cloak. *To work, young woman,* she reminded herself.

Taryn came out of the shack and stopped. Chip was in the truck. In the passenger seat.

"Hop in," Cowboy Man called. "There's room!"

"Can't he ride in the back?"

"He howls nonstop when he's back there—scares the livestock within hearing range. He'll be fine, you'll see."

Taryn eyed the animal warily. He looked harmless now, but her limbs still felt wobbly after her experience in the shack and she yearned for some recuperation time. "You know, I don't think I can take much more of the excitement involved with you getting me to the inn. How much farther is it?"

"Just another five minutes."

"Really?" This was good news.

"Really. You're not thinking of walking, are you?" He was leaning over Chip to talk through the open passenger-side window. Man and beast faced her expectantly.

"Actually, yes."

There was something pleasantly mesmerizing about the deep smoothness of his voice, the way he spoke, and definitely the way he looked—and looked at her. But he scattered her thoughts. It was a reaction with which she was both unfamiliar and uncomfortable. Breaking the stare with a jerk of her head, she moved toward the truck and dumped her things into the back. They couldn't get any dirtier than they already were, she reasoned.

Her emotions were raw; her life contained so much uncertainty and turmoil right now, making her too vulnerable to his unique brand of cowboy charm. She needed to restore some order in her life—an essential element for career success, she reminded herself—and that meant getting a handle on her emotions. A short walk through the last of the woods and down into Aspen Creek Valley would do a world of good to revitalize her and ground her back to reality. She was already late. How much difference would a few more minutes make?

"Could you please drop off my stuff?"

"It'll take you half an hour."

"I thought you said five minutes."

"Five minutes by truck."

"I'll risk it. It'll be the continuation of my afternoon adventure," she said sarcastically.

"Someone as accident prone as you shouldn't be wandering out here alone."

"You're not as amusing as you think you are, you know that? I'll be better off alone than with you. I've concluded that you're bad luck."

He looked at her for a moment, a warm smile on his face.

"Please get in," he said quietly. "I guarantee that nothing else will happen."

Despite herself, something inside her softened. Could any mortal woman resist an invitation delivered like that? "You can't guarantee that."

"If something else happens, I'll use my lariat to tow your car out today. How's that for collateral?" he challenged.

"I thought you said it would snap."

He raised his brows slightly and grinned. "Trust me."

Said the spider to the fly. Taryn glanced at her watch again. How late could she afford to be?

Moments later, remembering that 'resistance is futile'—a quote from a favorite science fiction film—she was bouncing along in the truck again. Cowboy Man had one hand on the steering wheel and one arm around Chip, who kept trying to lick Taryn's face.

"He's begging forgiveness," he explained.

Taryn grimaced and stuck as close to the door as possible. "He's forgiven, if he stays off me for the next few minutes. I'd really like to keep this outfit reasonably clean."

As they crested the last hill, she couldn't help smiling at the vista spread before her. The vast property of the Aspen Creek Inn and Ranch stretched through the valley. It was just as she remembered it when she visited her dear friend Alison here a few years ago. After the harrowing events of the afternoon, the thought of seeing Alison again gave her some comfort.

The lake's surface was a sheet of glass in the still, warm air. It cut a perfect S-shape through the sparsely vegetated valley bottom. At the first bend of the lake, the ground rose away from the rocky shore and became the inn's golf course, an oasis of manicured green creeping into the coarse sage, bunchgrass, and sprawling junipers surrounding it. A beach had been carved out of the shoreline at the far end of the golf course, closest to the inn. Squinting, Taryn could just barely make out a few people splashing in the water, a canoe, and the bright red of a windsurfer's sail hanging limp in anticipation of the next gust.

Across the lake from the golf course, a big red barn and other ranch buildings huddled against the first of several small, bench-like foothills. These rose step-wise on either side of the valley, gaining larger trees and other vegetation with altitude, to form high, forested plateaus reaching to distant mountain ranges. Taryn's gaze drifted back to the sprawling, Victorian-style inn commanding the shore at the top of the lake. Even from this distance she could see features which gave the structure some of its charm: covered porches, tall dormer windows, and a wide front stairway.

Taryn jumped out of the truck before it even came to a full stop in front of the inn. Collecting her few belongings, she said simply, "Well, thanks for the ride," thinking few words were probably best.

The handsome stranger smiled. He seemed to do that often, she noticed, and it suited him well. "I'll see to getting your car towed tomorrow."

"That would be great." Her every movement, every word, seemed distorted, mechanical. Why was this so awkward? "Thanks," she said again.

"See you around," he replied, tipping his hat.

She turned as he pulled away, thinking—hoping—he probably wouldn't be around the hotel much anyway. Cowboys stuck to the stables and the pasture, after all. She tried to put him and the afternoon out of her mind as she looked up at the inn, welcoming the wave of excitement, and even the nervousness, that came with the realization that she had finally arrived.

Chapter Two

The gleaming wooden floor creaked gently under Taryn's weight as she entered the inn. There was no one at the front desk or, she discerned as she craned her neck to see through the saloon doors, in the office behind it. The only sound was a lilting of women's laughter emanating from somewhere in the back of the building. She stood in the open doorway for a moment, a welcome breeze cooling her flushed cheeks and sending the foyer's lace curtains into a swirling waltz. The ornate oak spindles on the staircase before her gleamed with a recent hand-polish, the tell-tale scent of lemon oil hanging in the air. She closed the door, pushing her hip against the old, weathered beast before it clicked into place. Where was everybody?

Taryn looked to the right, through the etched glass window of the dining room door. Empty of people, the tables were all perfectly set with white tablecloths, red serviettes, and fresh wildflowers. Turning left, she walked through the parlor, zig-zagging around various overstuffed pieces of furniture and the huge antique piano that dominated the room.

The unseen women's laughter grew louder as Taryn neared the saloon, and with each step the rich aroma of coffee grew stronger. One pitch of laughter was especially familiar, and joy swelled in Taryn's chest as she entered the room and saw her dear friend perched on one of the plush bar stools, both elbows resting on the huge mahogany bar behind her, laughing with three other women. The worry, frustration, humiliation, and fatigue of the past few weeks were momentarily forgotten.

Alison stopped mid-sentence and slid off the barstool. "Taryn!"

Taryn's jaw dropped as she noticed her friend's swollen belly. "Oh for . . . Why didn't you say something? When did this happen?" she sputtered with delight.

The tiny brunette had already enveloped Taryn in a big hug. "Due in October—two months to go. I didn't want to tell you on the phone. Surprise!" She took a deep breath, holding Taryn at arm's length. "And I want you to be the godmother."

Taryn laughed, warmed and relieved by her friend's chatter. "Yes, I'd be honoured—"

"But we can talk about that later," Alison went on. "Did you get caught in the storm? Cripes, didn't that one pack a punch? Come, sit down." She steered Taryn to a barstool and continued her barrage of observations and questions.

Taryn gave Alison another hug, inserting quickly, "You have no idea how good it is to see you." She turned to the three women who were looking on quietly, their faces lit with bright smiles.

"Hi. I'm Taryn." She held out her hand to the nearest woman who gave it a hearty shake.

"I'm Margaret MacKay." She was a plump, robust, greying woman in her early sixties with rosy cheeks, twinkling blue eyes, and fans of crows' feet to prove a semi-permanent smile. Taryn liked her immediately, sensing in her a warm, motherly quality that was supported by the floral apron she wore. "Inn's housekeeper," she added. Taryn noted with pleasure the woman's Scottish accent. It was a light brogue that she had always found so pleasing.

"Oh gosh, I'm sorry." Alison clamped her hand to her heart in a gesture that, Taryn knew, meant she was socially mortified. "Introductions, of course." She quickly introduced Taryn to the other two young women, Tina and Susan, teenaged sisters whose jet-black hair, almond-shaped eyes, and tanned complexions suggested a native heritage.

"Aren't you supposed to be meeting with Fred?" Alison asked.

"I'm a bit late, actually. I should go find him."

"He'll be in the main office," Margaret offered. "I'll see you up to your room to freshen up, if ye'd like. Another few minutes won't make no never mind." She turned to Alison. "Ye'll need to be getting back to the club house. A carload of golfers just arrived."

"What?" Alison whirled around and craned her neck to look out of the window. "How do you do that?" Alison gave Taryn's hand a quick squeeze, and made her way to the door. "She's got a sixth sense, I swear. I'll track you down later, Taryn. Take good care of her Margaret!"

"That dear Alison is a whirlwind, no?" Margaret chatted on as she led Taryn up the wide Victorian staircase.

"Of the best sort," Taryn agreed with a grin as they continued down the hall of guest rooms and turned into the doorway at the end. It opened to a narrower staircase leading to what Taryn assumed were the staff rooms on the top floor.

"Nice man, Fred Bennett," Margaret said over her shoulder, leading the way. "Seventy-five years old if he's a day, but sharp as a tack. And that Douglas of his, such a nice laddie. I understand that ye two will be working together. That'll be lovely then. Oh my," she paused for breath halfway up the stairs, "such a long way, isn't it?"

Taryn agreed, slightly out of breath herself.

"We're so glad he could find someone as capable as you

on such short notice," Margaret went on as she reached the top of the stairs.

Taryn tried to beat down the tummy-ticking brought on by the mention of her co-manager. *Hopefully, this Douglas 'laddie' won't turn out to be a spoiled rich brat.* After what had happened at her last job, it was crucial that she put her best foot forward, right from the start. And at the moment her best foot felt rather delicate.

Margaret's huge key ring jingled as she sought the correct key to Taryn's room. "That first door off the stairs," she gestured with a nod of her head, "is the bathroom for this floor. The only people ye'll need to share that with are the chefs, Hans and Gertrude, who each have a room up here. Ye'll meet them later." She leaned over conspiratorially, eyes twinkling, and Taryn quickly looked over her shoulder to see if anyone else was around. The hall was empty. "Quite a pair they make," Margaret whispered. "Oh, the rows they have . . . but they can cook, I dare say." She laughed and went on. "The other two rooms are spares for staff that may end up working late on some nights, like the dining room staff. It can be a long drive home for some of them." She swung the door open with a flourish. "There ye are, dearie."

The open door revealed a square, spacious room, simply but brightly decorated. A colorfully braided rug stretched across a polished hardwood floor. Its patchwork pattern complemented a lumpy, comfortable-looking quilt spread across an iron-framed double bed. An antique princess dresser backed onto the wall to her left. The tall Victorian window stood open, its lace curtains quivering in the breeze.

"Wow," Taryn remarked as she walked in. How easy it would be to feel at home here, she thought suddenly. She thought back to the dozens of times she had moved in her lifetime—first as a child of divorced parents with joint custody, then for school, then for her career. She'd never actually stayed in one place long enough to really feel at home. But this . . .

Career comes first; the words came to her as she set her things down. *Build the career first, then find a place to call home. That's the smart way to do it.* She paused, the worn brass knob on the closet door catching her eye. The advice, quoted straight from her mother, somehow clashed with the old beauty of the simple fixture. She walked over and ran a finger over it. Only part of the etched pattern was still visible. She briefly wondered how many hands it would have taken to wear it down like that. Generations of hands, she suspected, and likely all from the same family. *Career first,* the advice pressed again. But wasn't her mother still searching, still wandering from job to job, without a real home, without roots?

She blinked the thoughts away and turned back to Margaret, noticing that the older woman was watching her expectantly. "Margaret, it's beautiful. I love it."

"I'm glad ye like it dearie, and I hope ye'll be comfortable here." Margaret smiled as she closed the door. "Likely we'll talk later."

After changing clothes again, Taryn ventured into the bathroom for a quick face scrub to ensure the last signs of the afternoon's mishaps were gone. It provided some restoration, as did the sight of the huge claw-foot tub and a silent promise to soak in it at the earliest opportunity. *This is feeling more like a home all the time.* A small giggle escaped her at the thought. Was fatigue making her giddy? She took a deep breath and mentally began preparing for her meeting.

The flutter in her stomach quickened its pace as she walked over to the ranch's main office. She looked out over the calm water of the lake, trying to absorb some of its stillness.

"That you Taryn?" a voice she recognized as Fred Bennett's called from an inner office as she entered the building. "C'mon in! We're in here. How are you doing? So glad you're here."

Fred Bennett rose from his chair and extended his hand

with a wide grin as she entered, making her feel immediately at ease. The table beside him was covered with maps and
notepaper. Another man was standing with his back to them,
filling his glass from the water cooler. The broad back and
the well-fitted jeans stopped her dead in her tracks, and the
smile froze on her face.

"This is Douglas Prescott." Fred turned and gestured
toward Cowboy Man, who turned around with his glass to
his lips, taking a long drink before flashing her a familiar
smile. "Douglas, this is Taryn Christiansen."

"I believe we've met, just briefly, earlier today," Douglas
stated with obvious amusement at Taryn's shock. "A formal
welcome, then. So glad you made it," he said with a wink.

Taryn forced her smile to stick—*just keep it in place until
you recover*—her eyes round with surprise. She didn't know
what to feel first; embarrassment that he may have mentioned to Fred the events of the afternoon? Betrayal of some
sort that he had not clarified just who he was? Why hadn't
he introduced himself? Had he known who she was?

Then there was that odd ticking in the pit of her stomach
as he looked at her. Taryn had never seen gray eyes look
anything but cold, but his were different; warm, striking
against his tanned skin and black hair. It was as if he could
see right through her, or read her mind. The thought made
her feel vulnerable, uncomfortable.

So this was the man with whom she had to manage the inn.
Her first management opportunity—the one that would set the
stage for her career advancement. Her whole career depended on success here. If first impressions were what they were
reputed to be, then she was off to a very poor start indeed!

She glanced at Fred, then back to Douglas, pulling herself
together and managing to utter in a controlled voice, "Oh,
yes, how nice to formally meet you." How had that sounded?
Rather professional, she thought. No tremor in her voice. No
clenched teeth. She tried to relax.

"Douglas here is going to help you out a bit—part-time, you know. I did mention that I'd get you some help, right?" Fred smiled and pulled out a chair for her beside his own and she lowered herself into it with a nod of thanks. Douglas pulled out a chair for himself on the other side of the table, spun it around, and straddled it in one fluid movement with an air of someone who was completely secure in his surroundings. Folding his arms on the back of the chair, his eyes found Taryn's again as Fred continued.

"We've always had couples running this place," Fred went on, "and I didn't want you to be too overwhelmed by it all, seeing as you're coming in when the season's already started— and you'll be giving extra attention to our marketing campaign."

"I appreciate your thoughtfulness," Taryn said evenly. "I'm certain we'll work well together." She almost frowned at Douglas as one of his eyebrows arched. She struggled for composure. If it was a challenge he wanted, she was beginning to feel up to it. "Does Mr. Prescott have much experience in the hospitality industry?" Taryn added, looking from Fred to Douglas.

"Please, call me Douglas," he said. "And, yes, I've had some experience running the inn."

They reviewed the details of the working arrangements for the next half-hour. "Enough for now," Fred finally said, pushing back his chair. "How about a grand tour? Douglas and I can show you around and you can get a better feel for the place." He came around her chair and eased it back as she rose. "And you can tell me more about those ideas you have for getting this place into the black."

The path they took was only wide enough for two. Fred walked beside Taryn and listened with avid interest as she described some initial blitz marketing ideas for the inn, while Douglas walked behind. They headed from the office back toward the inn itself.

"As I mentioned in the interview," Taryn explained, "I'm

planning an advertising campaign in Vancouver to market the inn as a specialty wedding location and as an executive retreat." She looked back at Douglas, who, to her surprise, nodded thoughtfully. She half expected him to do something to raise her ire again, but for the moment he seemed all business. "And I think we may be able to get a few golf tournaments going up here too," she continued. "I mean, you've got a population of almost two million people in the Vancouver region, just a few hours drive away, along one of the most scenic highways on the continent, and I think that's something you really need to tap into."

"That's just the kind of thinking that got you hired." Fred smiled. A row of young poplar trees lined one side of the path, and he held back a stray branch as they walked around it.

"Ironically, I did some research about the best places for wedding sites and executive retreats at my last job. It was a special project I took on, as the Stanley Park Hotel was interested in pursuing that market itself. It was right on the downtown waterfront at the edge of Stanley Park, with a great view of the harbor and the mountains. But the result of the research was that a downtown location was far less desirable for that kind of thing than a country inn, even when travel time is brought into the equation." Taryn gestured toward the lake, benchlands, and distant snow-capped peaks. "This type of setting simply came out tops in the final analysis."

Also ironic, she thought to herself, was the fact that the research was, indirectly, one of the elements involved in her resignation.

"We have to admit, Taryn, that we haven't spent much time on marketing activities," Douglas said. "Most of the people who've run the inn for the past ten years or so have been friends or family just trying to help out."

"Yes," Fred agreed. "We're a ranching operation first. The inn, as much as we love it, has always played second fiddle. It was once my grandfather's family home, you know, back when the family was huge and the ranch was three times the size it is now. It really only became an inn by default, when my wife—God rest her soul—decided to take it on as a personal project of hers." He smiled and briefly placed a weathered hand under Taryn's elbow in a gentlemanly gesture as they stepped over a rough part of the path.

Gravel crunched under their feet. She loved the sound, and tried to remember the last time she'd walked a gravel path. Looming before them, the inn was bathed in the warm glow of a late afternoon sun hanging low in the sky. A soft breeze rippled the lake's surface, shattering the sun's reflection into millions of watery diamonds. Taryn felt the peace of the earth, sun, and wind begin to chip away at the month-old knot in her stomach.

"Everyone's well-meaning," Douglas inserted again from behind them, as the path wove through the inn's garden area. "And we appreciate their efforts. But it's high time we had someone with some real training in this kind of thing."

A long row of huge rose bushes lining the back fence caught Taryn's eye as they rounded the corner of the building. Hundreds of pink blossoms glowed in the evening sun. She caught a bit of their subtle fragrance and inhaled deeply.

"Impressive, en't they?" Douglas remarked quietly as Fred stepped ahe d to get the gate. "They're Gordon's specialty. Margaret's husband."

She glanced at him in surprise—men didn't usually comment on such things, she thought—and nodded her agreement before turning her attention back to Fred.

"I don't think we've done much formal advertising," Fred paused and frowned, "ever. Just word of mouth mostly. I admit, I'm a little embarrassed to stand here and say that, and in the same breath complain that the place doesn't make any money." He gave her a sheepish grin. "But there you have it. Anyway, I'm glad you're here, and on such short notice." He turned to Douglas. "Speaking of short notice, have we heard from Ron and Jackie?"

She remembered Alison mentioning Ron and Jackie.

The couple who had run the inn earlier in the season had been expecting to celebrate the birth of their first grand-child. Instead, their daughter had had triplets. The new arrivals were more than the young couple had bargained for, so Ron and Jackie had gone to Vancouver to give them a hand.

Douglas nodded and smiled as he leaned over to latch the white picket gate. "Everyone's fine. Busy, but fine."

Taryn ducked around a renegade batch of clematis vines trying to escape a wooden trellis, the deep purple flowers bobbing in the breeze. She thought it strange that no one seemed to resent Ron and Jackie's sudden departure. "I don't mean to pry," she said to Fred, "but you don't seem very upset by their leaving at such an inopportune time. They must have really left you in the lurch."

Fred shrugged as he lead them towards the corral. "Well, getting upset over it wouldn't solve anything anyway. Wasn't anything we could have done about it. Those little babies needed their grandparents."

"Family comes first," Douglas added.

Taryn pondered that as they neared the stables, a little sur-prised at the simplicity with which Douglas stated the con-cept. In her mind, the matter was much more complicated than that. And in a case like this, the notion of family taking priority over career was foreign to her. She supposed that some families operated that way, but hers hadn't. She had always felt second to her parents' careers, but hadn't thought about it much—not enough to resent it, in any case. Work always came first because work provided for the family, for life. Of course, she conceded, if there were an illness in the family, that would be different. But for something like this? Couldn't just one of them have gone to help with the babies, leaving the other to fulfil their responsibilities at the inn?

"Besides," Douglas went on, "their sudden departure made us really take stock, and take notice. This season's prospects are less than stellar; advance reservations are down again. We need a professional. I took over for awhile to keep things moving while we found you."

"Everything happens for a reason, you see." Fred clapped her gently on the back, a friendly gesture that made her feel . . . accepted, somehow. "Don't get me wrong, though. I'm scared as hell about losing this place."

Douglas interjected. "Fred explained, didn't he, that if we don't do something to appease our creditors, we'll be in huge trouble come next spring?"

Taryn nodded solemnly as they entered the cool, dim interior of the stables. The strong, sweet smells of hay, horses, and leather—good, honest, earthy smells—made her feel grounded, steady, and real.

During her interview, Fred had told her up front the inn was in trouble, had been in the red for too many seasons now. Taryn remembered the tension in his old face as he explained how, in the past, the price of beef had been high enough for the ranching part of the family business to offset the losses of the inn. But the price of beef was on a slide. By the end of this season the inn had to break even, at least, and show some potential for a profit next year.

"They've given us a reprieve this year," Fred said, "some loose credit terms and such, but . . . well, we've got to prove a turn-around." He shook his head and Taryn's heart went out to him.

The wiry old man had kept this operation running for years. He was tough and weathered, Taryn thought, but he cared about people. She had sensed it in the initial interview. So many people's jobs depended on the inn, ranch, and golf course doing well. Without the jobs, the Aspen Creek community would disintegrate.

"We'll make it work, Fred." She gave him a confident smile, which he returned with a nod. She glanced at Douglas, who held her gaze with a curious, assessing look of his own. Gosh, Cowboy Man has glorious eyes, she thought again. To which she'd better build up a resistance, she told herself sternly. The man's gaze killed her concentration.

The tour ended back at the hotel's small office. Outside, dusk was settling into darkness. "Well, Taryn," Fred said, turning on the two big brass desk lamps. "We'll probably be talking more in the next day or so as you get settled in, but then I'm off 'til the end of the season, as I mentioned earlier."

Taryn's jaw dropped, but she quickly snapped it shut. "Ah, no, I don't remember . . ." He was leaving? She'd be here alone with Douglas? Well, not alone, really, but in terms of owner representation . . .

"Oh, I'm sorry. I may not have known about that when we talked last." Fred's brows creased. "It's the old ticker, you know," he sighed, tapping his chest lightly. "Never been one to laze around and let others take care of me, but the doc warned me to reduce my activities, reduce my stress, and get some treatments. Said I'm a heart attack waiting to happen. So, we'll see. Eight weeks he booked me in for; one of those health farm clinics. Might do me some good."

"As long as the nurses are pretty," Douglas added dryly.

Fred gave him a wink and a wide grin. "That would ease my burden, of course. Anyway," he turned back to Taryn, "Douglas has really been running this whole operation—the ranch *and* the inn—for the past few weeks, and sharing all the work with me for the past few years. The whole place will be his when I retire, after all. You can count on him if you need anything." Fred nodded at Douglas and clapped him on the back with a smile. "I think you two will make a great team. You take good care of Taryn here, Doug."

Douglas nodded. "I'm sure we'll make a great team and I'll take exceptional care of her. I've had good practice already," he added with a straight face.

Fred appeared not to notice that last comment, muttering something about his keys while digging in his vest pocket, but Taryn clenched her jaw, a betraying blush creeping into her cheeks. Douglas was baiting her again. She refused to bite. A huge task lay ahead of her and she needed to keep everything extremely professional. She felt as though her life were at stake here.

They looked at each other in the thickening silence that followed Fred's departure.

"Why didn't you tell me who you were this afternoon?" Taryn finally demanded, unable to keep the testiness from her voice.

"You never asked, and never thought to introduce yourself either." He slid into the polished oak chair and casually stretched his long legs.

"But you knew who I was."

"Pretty much." He leaned back, folding his hands behind his head.

She paused, putting two and two together and, with great effort, softened her tone. "And that's why you offered to stop at the old shack so I could get changed, instead of letting me wait until I got to the inn. It was only another few minutes away."

"I didn't think you wanted to show up at your new home looking like you'd just wrestled a steer in the mud," he smiled.

Rats! Taryn lowered herself into the chair on the opposite side of the desk. Indebted to him again. She didn't like it; it made her feel dependent. She preferred being angry with him. Anger somehow made it easier to demonstrate that she wasn't a push-over, that she was to be taken seriously. But he'd taken the bluster out of her sails. She couldn't be angry for too long. Good manners and simple professionalism dictated that she be grateful instead. It ate at her.

"That was thoughtful of you. Thanks," she managed.

"I've been known to be thoughtful, now and then." His eyes held hers. "Why does it bother you so much?"

"Why does what bother me?"

"My doing something for you. You're uncomfortable with it. Why is that?"

"I don't know what you mean," she lied.

"The look on your face just now, when you thanked me, was like you'd swallowed a stone."

The conversation was getting way too personal, but the gray eyes mesmerized her tired mind. "I'd just prefer not be indebted to you."

"You shouldn't feel that you are. Hypothetically though, why would *that* bother you? It's part of life. You know, give and take."

What could she say here? That anger made it easier to resist his charm? That would certainly move things from bad to worse. How could she get out of this conversation? Her brain tried to organize her muddled thoughts. "I'd just prefer not to count on other people for things that are important."

"A lonely way to go through life." He thought about it for a moment. "But you need others in order to do your job."

"That's different. That's work. People are paid to be dependable."

"Hmmm." His hand rubbed the faint stubble on his chin. "So, it's in your personal life that you find people aren't dependable?"

"Something like that." Was the answer vague enough that he'd take a hint and drop the subject?

"I don't think you'll find that here."

Was he suggesting she'd develop some personal relationships here? Before she could say anything else, he leaned over and casually tucked her hair behind her ear. She froze, her heart hammering like a wound-up drummer boy.

He leaned back with an easy chuckle. "You should see your expression now—a deer caught in headlights. Holy smokes, Taryn, just relax a bit, will you? It was just a curl gone astray."

Enough was enough. The ease with which he shot holes in

her composure was ridiculous. She took a deep breath and, for once, did what he suggested. She relaxed. A little. "Shall we get down to business?" She indicated the papers on the desk.

"You relax by working?"

"Maybe I do." Taryn tried to keep the challenge out of her voice. She didn't want to argue with him. She didn't want to be charmed by him. She just wanted to work with him, productively and in peace. Gosh she was tired. She blinked a few times, trying to remove the grit of fatigue from her eyes.

He eyed her curiously for a moment. "Alright then," he said, turning his attention to the mass of paper before them. "Tell you what. I'll clean up the stuff I've been working on and we'll start fresh tomorrow. Meet you here at seven. You've had quite a day." He gave her a small smile and added quietly, "Maybe you should just get yourself into bed, Taryn."

The gentle suggestion and the way he said her name really sent her emotions reeling this time. She dared not look up at him, knowing her face would betray the ease with which he could charm her. "Well . . ." she said, hoping to disguise her relief by absently moving the papers around on the desk.

A square, tanned hand gently reached out and covered her own on the desk. She felt his strength, and his gentleness, as he stopped her from shifting the papers. His head was beside hers now, and she could even feel the heat from his body. "I had that all organized," he said quietly. She heard the smile in his voice. "We can start tomorrow. Go to bed, Taryn."

She snatched her hand away and rose, stepping away from him and straightening her back with new resolve. "You're probably right," she said quickly, making her way toward the door. "See you at seven. We can start fresh then. Goodnight Douglas." She was already halfway to the stairs, trying to convince herself she wasn't running away, as his reply reached her ears.

* * *

Taryn jumped out of bed and crouched in the dark bed-room, panic gripping her body. It took a few seconds to remember where she was, but the realization did not ease her fears. What was that noise?

Creak, creak, creak. Loose floorboards in the hall near her door complained under the weight of someone's step.

The doorknob rattled and turned. Mind racing, Taryn tried to remember if she had locked it. Damn! Where was the light? Her hands flailed about the night table and something crashed to the floor. So much for the light.

"What the . . ." a muffled male voice sounded from behind the door.

Thank goodness! It must be locked! She moved her hands along the wall, looking for the overhead light switch.

Keys jingled softly in the hallway. He was coming in! *Forget the light, look for clothes!* Clad only in her underwear and camisole, she tugged at the quilt on her bed.

The lock turned. *Forget the clothes, look for a weapon!*

Taryn's heart pounded, the pressure of fear and panic making her slightly dizzy. Her ears rang. She prayed she wouldn't faint. The lock clicked. She found her shoe with one hand and jumped onto the bed, pulling the quilt up with her. The door swung open. Holding the quilt against her body, she raised her shoe and took aim.

A large silhouette could be seen against the bright light of the hallway. The man stepped into the room. Her scream caught in her throat, emerging as a pained croak, and she threw the shoe with all her might.

"Ugh!" He was quick, but not quick enough, and the shoe caught him in the ribs as he tried to side-step it. "What the hell . . ."

Taryn quickly grabbed the picture off the wall at her side and wound up to send it across the room in her best Frisbee toss. The figure from the doorway came hurling toward her, closing the distance between them before she could let loose. She cried out as he tackled her on the bed, knocking the wind out of her.

"Will you be quiet! It's me, Douglas, you maniac! What are you trying to do?"

His face was within inches of hers. His big, solid body pressed her into the mattress. He raised himself slightly onto his elbows and looked down at her, his expression one of bewildered amusement.

She shifted slightly in an attempt to keep the quilt in place over her body. Then her eyes locked with his, and for an instant neither of them moved. Then outrage and a substantial dose of fear quickly resumed their place at the forefront of her emotions. She pushed at him with her free hand. He was slow to move.

"Get off me right now!" Her voice rose to a screech as a spark of memory ignited—Todd, pinning her arms as she struggled to get away—searing her thoughts with renewed panic. She shoved with all her strength, hastening Douglas's retreat.

Douglas stepped back, holding his hands up in a show of innocence. "It's alright, Taryn. I'm off, I'm off. It's okay."

It's in the past, and Vancouver is a long way away. She doused the memory with her present anger. "What are you doing? Is this how you welcome new people? By sneaking into their bedrooms at night and scaring them within an inch of their lives? Get out of here!" She rolled herself in the quilt as she rose.

The overhead light flicked on, and a gasp from the doorway turned both their heads. Gertrude's hand covered her mouth in shock while Hans's arm lowered the baseball bat he had brought to assist the would-be victim. "What's going on in here?"

"All's well, Hans, just a bit of a mix-up." Douglas's voice was even, controlled.

"Everything's fine, Hans, Gertrude." Taryn attempted the

same tone, with limited success, giving Douglas a seething look before turning back to Hans and Gertrude. "I'm really sorry we woke you." The negative effect this would have on their impression of the new hotel manager was not lost on Taryn, and she groaned inwardly, wishing she could just click her heels and disappear.

Hans and Gertrude continued to stare, obviously uncertain as to what was going on, and what, if anything, they should do.

"Not to worry. You can go back to your rooms, really." Douglas said, waving them away.

The two chefs exchanged puzzled glances. "If you're sure . . . ?" Gertrude began.

"We're sure," both Taryn and Douglas said in unison.

With that they uttered distracted goodnights and made their way back to their rooms. The phrases ". . . young people . . . foolishness . . . I told you it was nothing Hans . . ." and ". . . *you* roused *me* from a sound sleep for this Gertrude . . ." floated behind them, finally silenced with the shutting of their respective doors.

Douglas frowned at Taryn, rubbing his side. "I'll bet I have the imprint of your shoe on my ribs, if you didn't crack one."

"You deserve worse." She raised her chin. "I'll bet I lost a year off my life, not to mention what Gertrude and Hans must think! You're lucky I didn't have a knife."

"I'll be sure never to give you one." He glanced around the room. "What are you doing in here?"

"What am *I* doing in here?" she sputtered. "I *was* sleeping." She jerked the slipping quilt higher around her body. "I think the question should be what are *you* doing in here?"

He looked at her for a moment, then let out a short, soft laugh. She raised her eyebrows, shooting him a derisive look.

"Sorry. The Goldilocks story just came to mind."

"What?" She frowned.

He shook his head. "Nothing. What's wrong with the bed in your room?"

The discussion was becoming increasingly frustrating. She crossed her arms and waited.

He laughed again, a deep, rich, even sound she noted—pleasant if the circumstances were different. "This isn't your room, love; this is one of the spare rooms, and tonight it's my room. It's too late to bother driving up to my place. Your room is next door." He made a sweeping gesture around the room. "Didn't you wonder why your stuff wasn't in here?"

Taryn looked around. It looked like her room. It was set up like her room, but the colors were slightly different and, true enough, her bags weren't here. She had simply been too tired to check. The hallway had been dark, the door unlocked. Bone tired, she had shuffled in, dropped most of her clothes, and crawled into bed. She felt the color rise in her neck, then her cheeks, and then her ears began to burn. She inhaled slowly. "Ruby red slippers," she mumbled, renewing her wish to disappear.

"I guess I can't be flattered if it was all a mistake," he quipped with a maddening smile.

She glared at him. Stiff-backed and silent, she picked up her clothes and retrieved her shoes. She marched out the door with lofty poise—or as close to that as she could get with the quilt dragging on the floor behind her. Once in the hallway she turned. "Well, maybe you should keep your door locked." Sadly, it was all she could come up with, but she said it with as much dignity as she could muster.

"May I just say that you look exceptionally lovely at this moment?" He was barely suppressing his laughter now. She could hear it in his voice.

"No, you may not. You may shut up." She spun around, gritting her teeth.

Balancing her belongings, she tried the door of her room.

Locked. *Groan.* She rested her forehead on the door and heard the dreaded sound—the jingle of keys from the doorway of the room she had just left.

"Here, you forgot your keys. Let me get that for you," Douglas said with mock gallantry as he unlocked her door, dropping the keys into her shoe. Bowing ceremoniously, hand outstretched, he bid her entry.

She stepped into her room and, in consideration of Hans and Gertrude, resisted the urge to slam the door in his face, quietly clicking it shut with more patience than she ever knew she possessed.

The man was going to drive her insane.

Chapter Three

Wrapped in her quilt, Taryn stood by the window in her room, watching the sun's first watery rays wash the valley in a hazy, pinkish glow. The lake shone like glass; the dawn air was damp and cool. In the distance, a lone rider cantered down the misty bench-lands. Resting her head against the windowpane, she briefly wondered at the chore that would have someone already returning at first light.

The storms in her heart had stilled somewhat during the night. She was blessed, she knew. Regardless of the awful things that had brought her to this point, she was lucky to be where she was now. She tugged at the quilt, securing it more snugly around her shoulders, and allowed herself a small, determined smile. Finishing off the summer season as manager of the Aspen Creek Inn would send her back to Vancouver well armed for other career opportunities. Not many twenty-seven-year-old women climbed the corporate ladder at this speed.

A sudden gust of wind shattered the lake's surface into a million glittering shards. *And that's how quickly life can change,* Taryn reflected. She thought back to her resignation from the Stanley Park Hotel. At the time, she'd feared that her bridges were burned behind her. But when she had gone to see her former manager to pick up her final paycheck, dear Aiden had offered her some hope. He made it clear that although his hands were tied regarding the promotion she'd lost, Taryn was welcome to come back to the hotel in the future. Coincidentally, Aiden's daughter had booked her wedding at the Aspen Creek Inn in September. He implied that he might even be ready to make her another job offer at that time.

Implied. Not promised. The offer was definitely going to depend on what he saw when he arrived at Aspen Creek. Taryn was determined that he would find fault with nothing.

She gave the slipping quilt another tug, listening contentedly to the subtle creaks and groans as the morning sun warmed the building's old wood. The inn was a charming contrast to the concrete world from which she'd come, but the Stanley Park Hotel had had its own appeal too. She'd loved her job there, and had been well on her way up the corporate ladder, climbing the rungs toward career success. It was everything she wanted.

Taryn grimaced and turned away from the window. She still couldn't believe it had turned out the way it did. Was she such a poor judge of character? Could she not have seen Todd would betray her?

She reluctantly unwrapped herself from the quilt and put on her robe. *Write it off to experience,* she thought bitterly as she began pulling clothes out of the closet. *No need to dwell on it anymore. His phone call was surely just an angry moment.* A blue cotton skirt landed on the bed, followed by a white blouse. He'd cool off and direct his energies at other pursuits, both personal and professional, and that would be the end of it. Pushing her feet into her slippers, she collected her clothes and toiletries and headed down the hall to the bathroom. A shower would definitely clear her head.

The thought of clearing her head led directly to images of Douglas. His effect on her composure, her emotions, was definitely unnerving—and unwelcome. She'd never met a man who could reduce her to such schoolgirl self-consciousness. It certainly didn't do anything for the persona of cool professionalism she fought to build and maintain as part of her career plan. And yet, reluctantly, she found herself wondering if he was just a handsome flirt or if was he really interested in her.

Stop! she told herself sternly. Handsome and charming as he was, he was a co-worker and, in Fred's absence, essentially her boss. Mixing business with romance was never a good idea, she knew that. She would steer her heart clear, keep her priorities straight.

A floral scent lingered in the bathroom. Taryn inhaled deeply. Roses, maybe jasmine, or gardenia, she guessed, spotting the potpourri-filled crystal bowl on the counter. The white claw-foot tub dominated the far end of the room. It was crowned with a brass ring, suspended from the ceiling, supporting a chiffon-like shower curtain now billowing in the breeze that had just kicked up through the open window. Now this, Taryn thought with a smile as she undressed, was a room where one could wash one's worries away.

Twenty minutes later, freshly scrubbed, her curls still damp, Taryn descended the stairs ready to face the day. She entered the small office from one end, just as Douglas walked in the other door, stopping her dead in her tracks. She couldn't help staring. He hadn't noticed her yet, and had obviously just come in from spending considerable time outside—lean cheeks ruddy, hair damp from the morning mist. She realized he must have been the rider she saw from her window. His jeans clung snugly, faded and worn in all the right places, she noticed in spite of herself. Whistling softly to himself, he unbuttoned his denim jacket, removed his cowboy hat, and expertly tossed first one then the other onto pegs near the door.

"Good morning," she said brightly, cringing inwardly as the breath caught in her throat.

He turned and paused, his gaze taking her in. "Good morning." As always, his deep voice was warm, his smile quick. He moved toward the desk, glancing at his watch. "It's not seven yet. Hope you slept well."

"Thank you, yes," she lied, sitting down neatly on her side of the desk. It was time to set matters straight. Right now. She took a deep breath. "I'd like to keep things on a strictly professional level—" she blurted out, instantly wanting to recall the words. Hardly cool and composed, she thought miserably. She exhaled slowly and tried again. "What I mean is . . ." She stopped. What she'd said was precisely what she'd meant. She let the sentence hang.

He didn't miss a beat, propping a booted foot on his chair, resting his elbow on his knee. "I see. A professional level." He paused, his expression thoughtful.

Taryn busied her hands by straightening a stack of papers on the desk before her. She had to regain the advantage—or rather, find it in the first place. Clearing her throat she raised her gaze to his, consciously stilling her hands, "I—or we, if you'd like to look at it that way—have taken on a huge responsibility here. There's no alternative but to succeed. I'd appreciate it if we could, somehow, put yesterday behind us and start from scratch today. As professionals. As co-workers."

"Taryn, are you embarrassed about yesterday?"

"Why, yes, of course," she admitted irritably. "Wouldn't you be?"

"Don't be." He sounded suspiciously cheerful. "In hindsight, it was all rather fun, don't you think?"

She refused to see it that way. "I'm . . ." She felt herself blushing, frustrated by her lack of finesse. "It wasn't very professional."

"There's that word again." She could feel his eyes on her. "You're finding this, ah, attraction, a bit distracting then?"

Damn him for pushing it, she thought. He was teasing her, entertained by her discomfort—and not for the first time.

"I really don't want to discuss that," she said, trying to be firm.

Douglas lowered himself into his chair, leaned back, and crossed his arms over his chest. "No problem," he said with a shrug. "I'll try if you'll try, Taryn. We are, after all, two responsible adults. We should be able to keep our desires at bay."

Desires! Now he was talking desires! Hardly helpful, and he knew it. His teasing strengthened her resolve. Did he think the cowboy had charmed the city girl into eating right out of his hand? A man like him probably mowed women over all the time. Now she was here, like fresh meat, new territory to conquer. Well, the past few months had taught her that she had to be vigilant. Her future depended on it.

She cleared her throat, deciding to simply ignore his last comment. "Let's get to work, shall we? The first thing I need to do is get my car and the rest of my stuff," she said stiffly, daring to look him in the eye.

He held her gaze for a long moment, a smile in his eyes if not on his lips, then nodded slightly as if acknowledging that the round was over.

Once they settled down to business, Taryn began to feel a little more at ease. Aside from a few breaks for phone calls, coffee, short conversations with staff, and greeting the tow truck with her repaired vehicle when it arrived, they spent the rest of the morning going over the inn's basic operating procedures. She had to hand it to him, he knew how the place worked, and he remained professional throughout the discussion.

"I'd like to experience some of the things the guests experience, to help me in writing my marketing material," she said as they made their way to the coffee shop for lunch. "You know, a few holes of golf, some riding, some trail walking." Now that he wasn't flirting or teasing her, she actually relaxed enough to enjoy his company.

He held her chair as she sat down. "Alison should be

able to link you up with some golfers. You can do a round with them and probably get a better feel for it than just going it alone." He sat down across from her. "Barrel does the rides. I'd be surprised if you could get him to talk much though." Douglas smiled at her questioning look. "A man of few words if ever there was one. And Margaret's husband Gordon is the expert when it comes to trail walking around here." He rose to pour two tall glasses of water from the pitcher on the counter, setting one down in front of her. "But let me know if you're not finding what you need."

They chatted easily as they waited for their orders, covering everything from unique guest preferences to the fact that Hans and Gertrude ran the kitchen and tolerated no interference. "Best just to leave it to them," Douglas advised.

"It must have been exhausting for you since Ron and Jackie left—you know, handling the work at the inn as well as your ranch duties," Taryn remarked between forkfuls of a delicious strawberry-spinach salad. In the strong light streaming in from the windows, the shadows under his eyes and strain lines around his mouth were plain to see. Sunlight was, Taryn reflected, ruthlessly unforgiving. She briefly wondered what she looked like in this light, then told herself it didn't matter one way or the other.

He shrugged. "Haven't been getting much sleep, but it's all got to get done. I've been through worse." He popped the last bite of a hefty ranch burger into his mouth. When he'd finished chewing he added, "I'd do just about anything for this place, for Fred." He pushed the plate away and leaned back in his chair with his coffee.

"I can see he means a great deal to you."

He nodded gravely, glancing out the window before adding, "He and Glenda raised me." He took a sip of coffee, squinting slightly as the breeze shifted the curtain and a shaft of sunlight splayed across his face.

Douglas, an orphan? "Did they?" She paused. Perhaps the

question was too personal, but out it came. "What happened to your parents?"

He took another sip of coffee. "Car accident. I was eight," he said, shifting his chair slightly to avoid the aggressive sunbeam. "Glenda was my mother's best friend. She and Fred took me in, brought me here to live with them."

"Glenda, Fred's wife, she . . ."

He shook his head. "Passed away about four years ago. Amazing woman, she was."

She stared at him for a moment, noting his matter-of-fact expression, the simple delivery of the tragic tale. It was obvious the grieving was over and the warm memories remained.

"I'm sorry." It was all she could say. She may not have had a traditional childhood herself, but at least her parents were always a phone call away, should she ever want to talk to them.

He gave his head a quick shake and smiled a bit, as if trying to break the sombre mood.

Taryn returned her attention to her salad, a bit surprised at the depth of that little heart-to-heart, but somehow not uncomfortable with it. They sat in silence for a few moments, Taryn chewing thoughtfully, wondering not so much about what he'd said, but rather why he'd said it to her.

"Good salad?" he asked casually.

She smiled and nodded before swallowing. "Anyway," she began, deciding to return to a less personal subject, "I guess it'll still be busy for you, doing your usual ranch work and keeping up with the inn's books in the evenings, even though I'm here."

He tipped his head back to drain the last of his coffee. "Whatever it takes, Taryn," he said, setting his cup on the table. "Be sure to let me know if there's anything you need. We've got to make this work."

The words brought welcome comfort. Although her confidence had returned, she appreciated his words of support. No matter how much he flirted or teased, it was clear that he took the inn and ranch business very seriously. She wondered if he knew that she'd had doubts about what she was getting herself into. Looking down to spear another tender strawberry with her fork, she also wondered if he generally knew more about her thoughts than he let on. The man seemed remarkably—and disarmingly—intuitive. It disturbed her.

"I'll try not to distract you too much," she promised.

"You already do, love," he quipped as he rose to leave, placing his cowboy hat firmly on his head. "In the nicest way, of course," he added in response to her puzzled look. The mischievous look from this morning had returned to his expression. "And I figure I do the same to you, so I guess that makes us even."

It was just as well he didn't give her a chance to respond; she couldn't think of a thing to say anyway.

Taryn was still at the table an hour later. Her notes formed a large fan before her, with more piled dangerously against the small crystal vase of fresh wildflowers that stood as a centerpiece on the crisp linen tablecloth. She looked up in surprise as a dainty hand rescued the tipping vase.

"Well, hello." She greeted Alison with a warm smile, then nodded at the vase. "And thanks."

Alison grinned and lowered herself, with remarkable grace considering the advanced stage of her pregnancy, into the chair Douglas had vacated. "So, are you finally going to tell me what happened at the Stanley Park Hotel?"

Taryn dropped her pen and leaned back for a stretch. "It's so good to see you too, Ali. I'm fine, thank you, and you?"

Alison waved her hand in mock dismissal. "Oh yes, hello, how are you, and now please fill me in," she replied with a laugh.

Taryn smiled warmly at her friend, reflecting on the fact that Alison was one of the few people she had kept in touch with over the years. The only child of divorced parents, Taryn and her mother had moved almost once a year, as her mother sought contract work as a management consultant, a field in which she was very successful. Taryn had attended more schools than anyone she knew, and lived in more hotels than she could count while they waited for a rented house or apartment to become vacant. When Taryn began college, her mother remarried and moved to Toronto with her new husband, and Taryn moved into student housing with Alison. Taryn had seen Alison only a few times since college—once when Alison married Tim, and again when Alison and Tim took over the management of the Aspen Creek Golf Course. They'd managed to keep in touch, though.

The two friends had the coffee shop to themselves. "Where should I start?" Taryn sighed. "Okay. You know we were both competing for the same promotion," she began.

"You and that Todd fellow?"

"Yep. And I didn't get it."

"That much I do know."

Taryn nodded again, giving her now-cold tea a thorough stir. "Well, I didn't know he was going for it too. He never said anything about it. I made no secrets about it to him." She laid the spoon into her saucer with a sharp clink, and looked up at Alison, resting her chin on her hand. "There was also another complication, in that he was interested in pursuing a romantic relationship, and I wasn't." She sighed. "When we first began working together, we went out for coffee once." She shook her head at the memory. "He was quite engaging from the start, and so insistent, I agreed to go, but . . . I didn't want to take it any further. I was clear about that, but he was pretty ticked off about it and just kept trying." Taryn grimaced and shook her head again. "Definitely not my type. And it's just such bad idea to date someone you work with."

"I'll keep that in mind," Alison grinned. "But since I'm married and pregnant, I don't think it'll be an issue for me."

"Right," Taryn said, too engrossed in her tale to respond to Alison's humor. She picked up her spoon and stirred again.

"Since you mention it," Alison began, raising her brows inquisitively, "have your interests run beyond work and career yet, Taryn?"

"To each their own, Ali. We're not all destined to be love-birds like you and Tim." Taryn rolled her eyes with a smile, softening the words.

"You're so gun-shy when it comes to *affaires de coeur.* I've never understood that, you being so beautiful and with no lack of opportunities."

Taryn shrugged. "Anyway," she continued, lowering her voice, "Todd gave me a ride home once. I suppose he thought he could win me over with the kiss to end all kisses. In the car." She screwed up her face in disgust at the memory. "When I rejected him, he got really angry and tried to stop me from leaving. I sure didn't see that coming." Down went the spoon again, nearly shattering the saucer.

Alison stared, wide-eyed. "And did you? Did you get out of the car okay?"

"I did, but . . ." Taryn absently rubbed her wrists, remembering the strength of his grip. "I was really afraid, Ali. The hard look in his eyes, when he said I led him on—which I did not," she added emphatically. "A complete stranger from the man I'd been working with."

Alison paled slightly and took Taryn's hand.

Taryn grimaced. "I was scared, but angry too—at myself, at him." She looked into Alison's eyes for the understanding she knew she'd find there, then smiled slightly. "And I did curse like a sailor at him, over my shoulder. Surprised myself even."

Alison smiled too, letting her continue.

"And so, the next day at work, things went downhill. That was expected, of course." She ran a hand through her hair and leaned back in her chair.

"I'm sorry."

Taryn shrugged. "Don't be. After that I began to see the *real* Todd. He'd never been a meticulous worker, more of a big idea man unwilling to sweat over the details that make a big idea work, but after that it got worse. He got so sloppy on our shift, making mistakes which he knew I'd scramble to correct, leaving early and forgetting to sign off on things so I'd have to do it—and he knew I would too. Since I was applying for that promotion I had to make extra sure everything was done properly." She pursed her lips, remembering.

"And then, on top of doing my work, and some of his, and looking out for his mistakes, I was also handed a research project. It was on the wedding and executive retreat markets. I was happy to do it, don't get me wrong, and I'd done several projects like that before, involving feasibility studies and such—but I had so much already."

"It certainly sounds like something you'd love to tackle," Alison remarked.

Taryn took a sip of tea. "Then, in an attempt to re-introduce some level of professionalism and efficiency to our working relationship—because things simply couldn't continue as they were—I discussed my resources, methods, and findings with Todd in a neutral, small-talk way, trying to include him in the project. But," Taryn smiled bitterly, "that backfired completely. In hindsight, I don't know what I'd hoped to accomplish with that, really." She carefully replaced her cup onto the saucer. "Pretty naive, now that I think about it."

"Don't be so hard on yourself. So he took credit for the project when it was done?"

"Not exactly, but good guess. After the project was completed, with the results showing that the hotel's style and location were good, but not optimum, for the market, I found out he got the promotion. He got the promotion I had worked for and deserved." Taryn felt her anger rising and clenched her fists. "Gosh, it still eats at me." She paused and took a breath. "I'm not sure if this had anything to do with it, but Todd casually took the results of my analysis, which were company property, and did some additional research of his own. He created an actual list of several properties in the province that would best suit the wedding and retreat market, and presented those together with some financial data. It was beyond the scope of my assignment, so I hadn't pursued that angle. Again, I don't know if that had anything to do with his getting the promotion, but . . ." Her shoulders slumped.

"He could have mentioned it to you. You could have included that in your report. It would have been easy enough to do, and would have make you look that much better," Alison finished.

"Exactly." Taryn nodded. "But it may not have made a difference. Todd had suggested to Aiden, our boss, that I had come to him for help on the project, that I was not ready for the position because I could not yet work independently on projects of that caliber."

"Unbelievable!" Alison snorted with disgust. "What a jerk. Why didn't you explain?"

"I didn't have a chance. I only found out later, by accident, from Aiden's secretary." She shrugged. "In the end, the reports were combined into one, with both our names on it, but getting credit for a report is really little consolation. And there's more," Taryn added, shaking her head. "I also found out that Todd is the hotel owner's nephew. Elliot Hagen runs Hagen Enterprises, the hotel's parent company. Imagine, in all the time we spent together, I never knew, and he never mentioned it!"

"Makes you wonder what else he hid from you."

Taryn gave an unladylike snort. "Some of the things I overheard on the phone were scary too. Like him talking with his stock broker." Her eyes widened at the memory. "The man either has a source of income that makes his hotel job completely unnecessary, or he has a level of debt that could rival that of a third world country."

"Seriously?"

"He's made a lot of bad deals, Ali." Taryn shook her head again. "Anyway, Todd's status at Hagen certainly explained why Aiden would be strongly influenced by him. And it really negated any effects that my explanations or protests—which would seem rather petty at that point—could have had on Aiden's decision. Aiden claimed his hands were tied by Todd's uncle. Todd was being groomed for head office work, and his uncle claimed he had to work his way up the ladder. With that kind of springboard under him, Todd doesn't have to work very hard to get to the upper rungs," she added sourly. "He just used me. And as the owner's nephew, he didn't even have to, which just makes it worse. I made it easier for him, easier than it already was."

"So you resigned?"

"Not quite." Taryn looked up from her cup. "Believe it or not, I was a sucker for just a little more punishment. Can you imagine how Todd behaved once he was in the new position? Within three days I admitted I couldn't work there anymore, not with Todd around, but I didn't want to ruin my chances of working elsewhere. I also didn't want to ruin my chances of working for the hotel once Todd moved to another rung on the ladder—which should be soon at the rate his uncle is moving him around in the company. So, it was a few more days of torture before I finally resigned."

"What a mess. What a jerk. You loved that job." Alison shook her head. "Is it any consolation that what goes around comes around? It's bound to, you know."

"Well," Taryn allowed herself a small smile, "there was a tiny bit of justice just after I resigned."

"Oh?" Alison gave her friend a wary look.

Taryn shook her head and smiled. "No, it wasn't anything too evil. Todd started pursuing an acquaintance, Tonya, who'd recently come into a hefty inheritance and was looking for investment opportunities. She worked for Hagen Enterprises. He began pursuing her within a week of my rejecting him, I might add."

"And?"

"We saw each other all the time at the gym so . . . Well, I just made a point of letting Tonya know of Todd's investment problems and, shall we say, *lack of chivalry* in the car that night." Taryn shrugged.

"Good for you!"

"She was shocked, to say the least. And she thanked me profusely for the warning. She's steering clear of him."

"And better off for it, I'm sure."

"Yes, well, she might be, but Todd put two and two together—or maybe Tonya told him about my advice to her. I don't know."

"Meaning what?" Alison's frown was quick and deep.

Taryn frowned too, remembering his reaction. "He called me the day before I left Vancouver to come up here."

Alison winced.

"He was so angry, like he was in the car that night. He said I betrayed him, that I ruined a huge deal for him and that he'd not only get me back, he'd also see me make it up to him."

"Black smoke. A man scorned. It'll clear." Alison waved it off.

Taryn nodded. "I guess so. Then he just hung up on me. The next day I left for here."

"He was just venting, blowing off steam."

"He did tend to be that way, you know, rather emotional

and explosive, but fairly quick to cool down once the moment passed."

"It's over. You're here now. New beginning."

Taryn took a deep breath and emptied her teacup, setting it down with finality. "You're right. And I've put it behind me." Ready to change the subject, she asked, "Did I tell you that Aiden Randolf, my former boss, will be here in a few months for his daughter's wedding?" Taryn went on to explain her optimism about Aiden's insinuation that her future employment back at the hotel would be influenced by what he saw during the wedding weekend. "Ali, I want that job even more now, maybe because of the way it was taken from me, but I want it badly."

"But I want you to stay here," Alison lamented, leaning back in her chair.

"Alison, my contract is only until the end of September, when the inn closes for the winter."

"Phhht," Alison intoned as she waved her hand, dismissing the comment. "Don't you think Fred will extend your contract once you bring this place into the black?"

"Into the black in one season would take a miracle! Our goal right now is just to break even for this season, and hopefully show potential for a profit next season."

"Details, details," Alison gibed. "Anyway, there's been talk for years about a winter opening—Christmas to Valentine's Day. That's when the snow's best. There's some great cross-country skiing around here during that time."

"Well . . ." It was the first Taryn had heard about the idea. "Let's just see how we do over the next couple of months, shall we?"

"Besides," Alison leaned over the table and whispered, "has your eyesight deteriorated since college?"

"My eyesight?"

Alison tilted her head, gesturing out the window. Taryn turned to see Douglas walking toward the inn with what she had already noticed was his characteristic long, strong, stride. Her heart stopped for a split second, and she exhaled slowly, trying to sound nonchalant. "Oh, him."

"Yeah, 'oh him,'" Alison mocked Taryn's tone. "Cripes, are you blind? The man is gorgeous. A hunk. Mr. Beefcake—"

"Oh, alright already!" Taryn laughed. It felt good. "He's very attractive, yes. He's also my co-worker and, in Fred's absence, my boss. From the frying pan into the fire . . ." Taryn paused, giving Alison an exaggerated accusing look. "And listen to the pregnant woman with the raging hormones. I thought you were happily married. Shame on you."

"Married, but not dead. No harm in looking. C'mon, Taryn, he's perfect. I'll vouch for his character. He's a perfect gentleman, loyal to his family and his home. Just look how hard he's worked over the past while, trying to run the inn on top of his other duties."

"Very noble, I'll admit. But you sound like you're trying to sell me something. I'm suspicious. If he's so great, why hasn't someone clicked with him yet? Hmmm?" Taryn raised her eyebrows challengingly.

"Oh, someone had. Unfortunately. They were engaged, briefly, and then she left him."

"Left him?" Taryn's jaw dropped.

"It's amazing he hasn't turned out to be a bitter person," Alison continued. "Her name was Carla. She was from Weston, a small town in the next valley. They met one summer about seven years ago after they both returned home from different universities. Got engaged in less than a year, sort of whirlwind thing. Had him working in Vancouver for awhile too, to be near her. He's a certified accountant too, you know," she added.

"An accountant-cowboy. Yes, I know. Interesting combination," Taryn remarked dryly.

"You'd be surprised at what it takes to run a ranch these days. Anyway, I digress. They set a date for their wedding, and then, a month or so before the big day, she just left. She went back to university to get her law degree and called him from there, letting him know the wedding was off. Can you believe it?"

"That's awful. What was the problem?" Taryn raised her hand to stop Alison's response. "Like it's any of my business. Never mind, I don't want to know."

"Well, I'll tell you anyway, because it'd be good for you to know." She paused to finish her tea. "They never really seemed that close, except right after they met. They hardly knew each other, I think. They had totally different interests. For one, she worked at the inn and hated it. In fact, she seemed to hate everything, and everyone. After a while, they didn't come to any local gatherings anymore because she would always be criticizing everything, saying it was all so small-town." Alison rolled her eyes. "Of course it's small-town. That's why we live here, for heaven's sake! It embarrassed him, as you can imagine."

Taryn nodded. "So one day she just left?"

"Oh no, not really," Alison turned her teacup in its saucer, an idiosyncrasy Taryn suddenly recognized from their college days. "She complained enough that he agreed to join her in Vancouver and work there for awhile. But it didn't work out at all. For one thing, he was home every weekend to help with the ranch. And when Glenda became sick, he quit his Vancouver job and came home for good, helping Fred care for her. His commuting was reversed. He tried to get into Vancouver on the weekends to see Carla. We were all relieved, in one way, when she agreed to come back. That's when they set the wedding date. But she wasn't here more than a month before she left for good. It wasn't the life she wanted. I can understand that part, but the way she made that clear to him, just plain leaving, was brutal."

Alison shook her head. "He didn't have too much time to think about it though, because Glenda took a turn for the worse about then, and Douglas spent a lot of time tending to her. Glenda was a mother to him—you know she and Fred raised him, right?—and her passing was as hard on him as it was on Fred, I think." She paused, taking a deep breath and looking up from her teacup.

Taryn remained silent, absorbing the tragic tale.

Alison made an attempt at a smile. "Anyway, since then, running the ranch and the inn has had him working eighteen-hour days. That may have saved his sanity. He's back to his old self now, you know, the way he was before Carla, and, if I may get back to my point, a walking definition of a hunk." She looked at Taryn thoughtfully. "I don't think he's taken an interest in anyone since Carla. Hasn't had time, for one thing, I guess. But he seems to have warmed up to you quite quickly."

Taryn shook her head, lowering her voice. "I'll admit, he does affect my concentration, but I can't risk any kind of emotional involvement. I need to rescue my career, and this is where I need to do it. Business and romance don't mix."

"When's the last time you had any kind of romantic relationship?"

"A few years ago."

"How many is a few?"

"Never mind. A few."

"Four, five?" Alison pressed.

"Okay . . . just under six years. Since college."

"Ah ha! You've counted back." Alison crowed in triumph, then stopped short and frowned. "Really? That Raymond fellow was your last boyfriend?"

"Pretty much. Twice over the years I've ended up dating coworkers—not at the Stanley Park Hotel, but at other jobs—and," she shook her head, "I tell you, Alison, when they say romance in the workplace is a bad idea, they mean it. It's just complicates everything, and makes for a very awkward—if not impossible—working environment, especially when the dating relationship ends, and even worse if it doesn't end by mutual consent. I'm never doing *that* again. My career is too important to me."

"Any great kissers?"

Taryn smiled. "The heart of the matter, is it? Well, there were no fireworks or anything, but one was—" she paused, searching for the right word. "Agreeable."

"Agreeable?" Alison pressed her fingers to her temples and shook her head. "Oh cripes."

"Nothing wrong with agreeable," Taryn defended.

"Regardless," Alison resumed, "the point is that you *have* counted back six years. When did you do that, last night when you couldn't sleep?"

Taryn eyed her friend warily. "What? Are you reading my mind now?"

"We pregnant women have remarkable intuition. You're destined, sister."

Taryn laughed. More relaxed now. "I'm not, but, just in case, I'll make sure I don't spend too much time alone with him."

Alison shook her head, a sad smile replacing her easy grin. "You're cheating yourself, Taryn. You don't know what you're missing."

The alarm clock's annoying shrill shattered the morning stillness. Taryn jumped from her seat at the window and turned it off. She had been up for an hour already, working at the small desk she had brought in, taking moments to stare out over the lake and hills as the sun infiltrated the mist, its early warmth an indicator that the day would be another hot one.

She had just seen Douglas ride out from behind the barns, heading into the hills. The image was now etched into her memory, like a scene from a favorite movie. His horse kicked up dust just outside the corral gates as it moved into a smooth, easy canter, splashing through the little creek at the base of the first hill. Douglas moved fluidly with the horse, relaxed, confident, his denim jacket flapping slightly at his sides, one hand on the reins, the other holding his lariat. Even from this distance, he cut a romantic figure, one conducive to thoughts of unbridled freedom and adventure. When was the last time her days consisted of either? she thought wistfully, then turned back to her paperwork.

Mornings in her room had become precious times of reflection, something for which she'd never taken time before. But then again, the view of the street from her little apartment in Vancouver could hardly compare with the one before her now. And she'd always been in a rush to join the morning commute. Now her only delay in getting to the office was, perhaps, chatting with hotel guests on the stairs. She smiled at the comparison.

A bald eagle, a frequent morning distraction, caught her eye. "Out for your breakfast, are you?" She watched it soar over the lake in a long, graceful circle, its sharp eyes seeking the flash of silver near the surface that would signify its next meal. Taryn had seen it dive just days before; an awesome combination of speed, strength, grace, and precision as the deadly talons ripped the unsuspecting trout from the water. She waited for a few moments more, hoping for a repeat performance, but her feathered friend continued to float through the air. "Slim pickings this morning, I guess," she murmured, and began gathering her paperwork and readying herself to go downstairs. "Glad I don't need to pluck my breakfast out of the lake," she laughed to herself, surprised at how easily the laughter came these days.

She checked her hands and her smile when she came to the file of completed work Douglas had given her last night. Douglas. The one element of her work here at the inn that continued to unsettle her.

The past few evenings Douglas's schedule had allowed him an hour or two in the office with her, keeping the inn's books in order. Although Taryn had her own space on one side of the desk, she found it difficult to concentrate on her work when he was there. The man seemed to overwhelm her senses. He still flirted with her but, worse yet, he challenged her. He pulled her into conversations that often had nothing to do with work. And, although hesitant, she participated—it was difficult to avoid, given that the man sat directly across the desk from her. She managed to quash any qualms she had about their rather personal discussions by telling herself that chatting with him was the best way to desensitize herself to his charm. And one of her mother's favorite sayings sprang to mind as well: *keep your friends close, and your enemies closer.* Not that he really represented an enemy, of course. But, however unintentional on his part, he did pose a type of threat. His presence managed to chip away at her sense of professionalism, her rules, her decisions about her life's direction. He wasn't doing it deliberately, she knew. It came from within her, triggered by, well, *him.* And that bothered her. Getting to know him better, his flaws and less desirable qualities—she was certain some would turn up—might just help her build some kind of immunity.

Taryn went to hang up her robe, chewing her lip as she reviewed their encounter two evenings ago.

Douglas had joined her, sitting down with a greeting and one of those quick smiles that made her toes curl. He bent directly to his work. Within a few moments, however, came the question, "What's the most romantic movie you've seen?"

Taryn blinked in surprise. *"Sleepless in Seattle,"* she answered off the top of her head, like a student suddenly the victim of a pop quiz.

"Hummm," he replied, without looking up.

Alright, she thought, *I'll bite.* "Yours?"

His pencil continued to move. He answered without pause, *"The Quiet Man."*

She thought for a moment, then remembered the classic flick with John Wayne and Maureen O'Hara. *"That's* the most romantic movie you've ever seen? John Wayne's character was completely overbearing!"

Douglas stopped working and gave her another smile. "Well, he had to be. Maureen's character gave more than she got. She needed a strong hand to keep her on track, don't you think?"

That got Taryn's back up. "No, I don't think." And so the debate began. "Keep her on track? Is that what you think strong-willed women need?" She couldn't tell by his expression if he was purposely trying to rile her, but her need to defend her gender was stronger than her desire to keep things strictly professional this evening.

"I didn't say that. But I do think the chemistry between them required the position John took. Otherwise that sweet, hot-tempered Irish siren would have walked all over him, and where would that have gotten them? He had to take the upper hand."

"Hmmmph." She refused to give on that point. It probably reflected his philosophy about relationships between the sexes, she thought. He was definitely the dominant male type. "It still doesn't get my vote for a romantic film, not even top ten."

"Well then," he leaned forward on the desk, propping himself on his denim-clad elbows, "let's look at your choice. Personally, I think Tom Hanks's character was too slow to realize that the woman he was dating was not a good match for him. I mean, what the heck was he doing with her? His son didn't even like her."

"He was grieving," Taryn defended. "And he hadn't even met Meg Ryan's character yet."

"No, but he'd seen her, just briefly of course, and those encounters rocked his soul. You could tell. He didn't know who she was, but when he looked at her, something sparked. How many times do you think that happens to someone in a lifetime? If you ask me, he didn't try hard enough to pursue her."

"So, you're saying you believe in love at first sight?" she teased.

He looked thoughtful for a moment, searching her face. "I'm saying that sometimes a man can have a good woman just about land in his lap and still not see the light." His voice softened as he added, "and vice versa, of course."

It took a few moments before she could break the eye contact. She looked down at the file folder in her hand, closed it, and opened another. She could feel the weight of the words he just spoke hanging in the air between them.

"What, no retort?" He rose then, came around to perch on her side of the desk, sliding some files into her in-basket. "Finished with those."

He seemed to loom over her. She felt as though she should stand, but had no reason to do so, other than a refusal to let him intimidate her. But giving in to that would be an admission of it, her thoughts collided as he prompted her.

"What is it about the movie that you find so romantic then?"

How did I get roped into this? She thought about his question for a moment. "It's poignant, tender. The characters' desires and fears are so real, so touching. The story just tugged at my heart, and then, well," she shrugged, trying not to sound sheepish, "it all turned out happy in the end."

As she finished, his arm reached toward her. "Hold still," he said, needlessly as it turned out, since she'd frozen on the spot. She felt a gentle stirring at her earlobe as he touched her earring.

"Relax, will you?" he said softly. "I just noticed that your little gold heart had flipped upside down and stuck. I'm not going to jump on you." He patted her hand and rose to pull open a file drawer behind her. "So, it's a poignant, tender romance you like then? The struggle for a happy ending?"

Way too personal, she determined. *Back out now.* Her earlobe still tingled from where he'd so gently touched her. "I just said that's what I liked about the movie. It wasn't a statement of my personal philosophy. I don't think it would be professional to discuss such personal preferences with you, in any case."

"Back to that are we?" he asked, with just a hint of sarcasm and a shrug, as he returned to his chair. "I just figured you'd enjoy in movies what you'd enjoy in real life. I find that's how it is with me."

The phrase "dominant male" sprang to mind again, along with some marvellously disturbing images of how beautifully the man fit the part. She had taken that as a sign that she'd better make some excuses and head upstairs with her work if she hoped to get any more done.

That had been two nights ago. Shaking the memory from her head, Taryn moved away from the closet. The man posed a challenge, to be sure, she told herself for the hundredth time, plopping herself down on the bed. She kicked off her slippers and pulled on her socks. He was a challenge that was far too charming, one against which she had little ammunition. In this case, getting to know the enemy wasn't helping matters much.

She tied the curtains back and paused to stare out the window as last night's discussion sprang to mind.

He'd asked her if she had any siblings, to which she simply replied, "No, only child," without looking up.

There was a long pause, which she eventually felt obligated to break. "And you? Any brothers or sisters?" He hadn't mentioned any when they'd talked about his parents during their recent lunch.

"Just Fred, no one else," he had replied, his fingers moving over the adding machine keys with practised ease. After a moment he stopped and added, "I would think that someone like you probably had one of those perfect childhoods—you know, parents could deny you nothing." He rested his hand on his chin, eyeing her expectantly.

She held his gaze for a moment, then busied herself with reloading her stapler. "Perfect? No, it wasn't quite like that," she said with a grimace.

Within minutes he managed to pull the details of much of her childhood and family relationships from her. She had to admit that she enjoyed surprising him with a life that was so very different from what he had obviously presumed.

He watched her intently as she talked, eyebrows raising from time to time.

"Only child, divorced parents, no roots, no home," he summarized. It sounded awful when he put it that way, and she felt her heart give a little lurch. "It sounds rather lonely," he added. "Perhaps even more reason to settle down and create something a little more traditional, more permanent?"

"Oh, I don't think that's for me." She shook her head.

"Well, it's got to be the right person, otherwise it's hell," he stated flatly.

The comment had made her uneasy, sending her thoughts in all directions. "What about you? I heard you were engaged," she said, trying to steer the discussion away from herself.

She was instantly sorry. His expression closed into a cynical half-smile and he ripped the tape off the adding machine with more force than necessary. "Well, that was a mistake." He seemed to shake it off immediately though, rising from his chair. "I'm getting a coffee. I'll bring you a tea," he said as he headed for the door.

Apparently there was still some bitterness there, she thought, remembering Alison's words about how Douglas was apparently "over it." He obviously didn't show this side to everyone. For a fleeting moment Taryn entertained the thought that he still had some feelings for his ex-fiancée. After all, he appeared to have had little choice in ending it.

The familiarity of their evening discussions made it difficult to maintain what she called work mode, that cool, composed concentration that allowed her to work efficiently. He wasn't purposely trying to undermine her management, she knew. His was just a natural charisma, particularly potent in the evenings when they were alone in the office. Perhaps the fatigue of the day made her more vulnerable in the evenings. Whatever the reason, there was only so much de-sensitizing she could take. After an hour or so in the office with him Taryn would bring her work upstairs. And he never questioned her about it.

In all her life she had not felt that kind of magnetism. She thought back to her college boyfriend. He had been a kind and giving person, and she did not regret the relationship, or ending it. They'd parted amicably, with a mutual understanding that the relationship had run its course, that it had nowhere left to go, really. But there certainly had not been the allure, the almost uncontrollable draw she felt when she was near Douglas.

Taryn was pulled out of her reverie by the chatter of red-winged blackbirds, starlings, and sparrows fighting over the kitchen scraps Hans tossed into the gardens every morning. It was a good thing, she reminded herself as she left her room, that she led her life with her head, not her heart. She had a career to re-build, after all, and day dreaming about a cowboy was not on her road to success.

Minutes later, covered in sunscreen, sporting a baseball cap with the logo of Vancouver's minor league team and riding boots borrowed from Alison, Taryn followed the aroma of strong coffee and freshly-baked blueberry muffins into the coffee shop. If she was quick, she'd have just enough time for breakfast before meeting Barrel for her ride.

"Good morning Margaret." She leaned over the counter, plugged in the kettle, and grabbed a cup for her tea, eyeing the tray of muffins Gertrude had set to cool. Only four remained. One of these days she was going to be too late, she thought with a smile, choosing one and sliding into a chair beside Margaret.

"Ah, good mornin' lass," Margaret leaned around the

table to look at Taryn's feet with raised brows. "Today's the riding day, then?"

Taryn nodded, a mouthful of heavenly flavor preventing speech. "With Barrel," she said, once she'd swallowed. "We'll be gone all morning."

Margaret's brows creased slightly. "Barrel? He just left for town, lass." She looked thoughtful, then added, "But Douglas was in here a while ago, whistling a happy tune. He was heading for the stables, last I saw. Perhaps . . ." she pursed her lips, eyes suddenly taking on a twinkle. "Perhaps he'll be seeing ye out today," she smiled into her coffee cup.

Taryn quickly stuffed another chunk of muffin into her mouth before anything untoward emerged. Riding with Douglas? Alone? In the hills? All morning? Her stomach began that now familiar ticking, but Margaret's next words interrupted further deliberations on the topic.

"By the by, a gentleman's called for ye twice already this morn', but he wouldn't leave his name."

The muffin stuck in her throat. Taryn swallowed hard, trying not to choke. It could be anybody, she told herself. Why the instant panic?

"Did he say he'd call again?"

"As a matter of fact, he did. And I'll bet," she cocked her head towards the door leading to the office, "that's him now. Very persistent, he seems."

Taryn had also heard the ringing of the telephone. She rose to unplug the kettle just as Tina stuck her head in the door.

"Ah, you're here. Phone for you, Taryn."

Taryn nodded her thanks and walked into the office on legs suddenly filled with lead, her boots dragging like dumbbells.

"Taryn Christiansen," she said into the receiver.

"Did you really think I wouldn't call back?"

She flinched as Todd's crisp voice snapped in her ear like the crack of a whip.

Chapter Four

Keep *it cool,* she told herself. "Good morning Todd, what can I do for you? I was just on my way out the door."

"It's about our unfinished business."

"We don't have any."

"There's some at this end," he replied sourly. "Your nosing into my business with Tonya cost me at least a hundred grand. I needed that money. I've got bills to pay and a big deal pending."

"If you don't get to the point in ten seconds I'm hanging up. I thought I made it clear I don't want anything to do with you."

"Fine." The word snapped over the telephone line. "I meant what I said about you making it up to me. I've made the arrangements."

"I'm not doing anything for you. You accosted me. You betrayed me. I owe you nothing." Her voice remained even, though her nerves were beginning to jump. *He's over three hundred miles away. He can't touch you.*

"Desperate times call for desperate measures. You can help, and you will."

"I'm sure I don't want to know, but why are you so desperate?"

67

Silence.

She caught on. "Your creditors are after you. It has nothing to do with me."

"You're already involved. I've set it all up."

"What?" She stretched her leg and nudged the office door closed as a knot formed in her stomach.

"You see, I knew I could count on you. I need you to give me some financial information about the inn, and Thompson Trust, the inn's creditor. I hear both are on the skids. Just give me that and I'll do the rest. I'm looking at a buy-out."

"What the hell are you talking about?" Her breath caught in her throat.

He laughed. "I knew that'd get your attention. See, it's not a big task on your part. And it's the least you can do after breaking my heart and ruining my chances with Tonya."

"Why would I ever, in a thousand lifetimes, do such a stupid thing?"

"Because if you don't, I'll blow the whistle on your being the leak that lost Hagen its buy-out of the Galiano Island property."

Taryn frowned, remembering quickly the corporate disaster a few months ago when Hagen suddenly lost its bid to buy a lucrative resort on one of the gulf islands off the coast. The corridors had echoed with rumors that someone at Hagen had leaked information to Staylander, another hotel chain. Staylander bought the resort right out from under Hagen's corporate nose.

"Me? I wasn't."

He barked a laugh. "No. I was." He let that sink in for a second before adding, "But it could look like you were. I've done some careful paperwork. I used your office security codes for a couple of my transactions. And there were those things you signed off on when I was out of the office—like courier packages. You're in there, Taryn. One of the advantages of being so conscientious in covering for me. But if you help me, I can clear your name if anything comes down."

Shock momentarily silenced her as she sank into the chair beside the phone. Then anger took over. "I won't be threatened, Todd. Or manipulated."

"If you follow this nice little plan I've devised, everything will be alright."

No! She shook her head. "I'm not participating. You can threaten me from now until the cows come home."

"A local expression? Cute," he said snidely. "I wouldn't need your participation if you hadn't blown it for me with Tonya. If I can pull off this buy-out, my uncle will promote me to a nice fat salaried position in the ivory tower. And more credit. I can pay my bills and save my investment deal. I won't need Tonya's money."

"No." She knew she should have hung up right then.

"If you don't do this for me, your career is shot, even if, in the long run, you could prove your innocence. Your reputation will be ruined."

"You wouldn't dare." Growing fury choked her response for a moment. "Besides, I could always clear my name, because I'm innocent. And if I did what you asked—not that I would in a million years—where would my career be then?" Why was she even discussing this with him? Her stomach began to churn and cramp. She squeezed the receiver to stop her hand from shaking.

"If you do this, I'd make sure to find a good job for you somewhere at Hagen, for as long as you wanted."

"As if I'd ever trust you! And it's not an issue anyway. I'm not playing. Get help, Todd. And don't ever call me again." With a wobbly hand she returned the receiver to the cradle and stared at the wall.

He's bluffing. She repeated it to herself over and over again. He couldn't possibly think such a stupid scheme would work. The more she thought about it, the crazier it seemed. He wouldn't dare! He was just blowing off steam again. And yet . . . she couldn't help wondering if he was desperate enough.

She made her way outside into the bright sunshine, trying to convince herself—no, remind herself—that if worse came to worst, she could take anything he threw at her.

Chapter Five

With a troubled heart, Taryn made her way along the path to the barns. She tried to concentrate on her steps, the boots unfamiliarly heavy on the crunchy gravel. *No,* she told herself again. *He's just trying to scare me. He's still angry. Sour grapes. It'll blow over. You've got to get past this and focus on the tasks at hand!*

The morning sun soothed her battered spirit. She lifted her face to it, trying to absorb its restorative warmth, as she crossed the huge corral. A pouch containing her sunglasses, a bottle of water, her camera, and a notebook bounced at her hip. The sweetly pungent smells of hay, leather, and horses filled her nose, growing stronger as she neared the stables. She stopped in the doorway, allowing her eyes to adjust to the darkness within. The cool inside air tingled on her bare arms.

"Barrel?" she called cautiously, stepping into the dim interior and looking around. Horses snorted and whinnied at her presence, and she stayed far enough away from their stalls so as not to be kicked by a nervous hoof. That much, at least, she knew. "Barrel," she called again. "Are you here?"

71

"Over here in the back," a voice called out from the far end of the barn. She didn't know Barrel's voice well, but she knew that wasn't it. A trickle of apprehension rolled down her back like a single drop of ice water.

"What are you doing here?" she asked as she came to the last stall where Douglas was working with the bridle of a huge black horse.

"I work here, same as you." He gave her a quick grin, taking in her appearance. "You look great," he added.

He didn't look so bad himself, she thought. He wore his trademark faded jeans. A soft denim shirt accentuated the gray of his eyes, even in the dim light of the barn. His rolled-up sleeves revealed strong, tanned forearms, dusted with black hair. "Where's Barrel? He's supposed to take me on some trails today."

"He's gone into town to get some medicine for one of the horses. I'll be taking you out today." He adjusted the bridle on his horse. "Easy now," he soothed. The animal shook its head and took a few steps back out of the stall. Douglas rested a hand on its neck, speaking quietly to it, settling it almost instantly.

Taryn backed away—both from the calm announcement that he would be taking her on a ride this morning, and fear of the huge animal.

"Perhaps I should wait for Barrel." The idea of riding in the backcountry alone with Douglas was more of a distraction than she'd bargained for. But then again, what was she really afraid of? That she'd succumb to his flirtatious country charm and throw herself at him? Hardly.

Douglas came out of the stall and pushed his hat back slightly with his fist. "Now why would you rather go with Barrel? You know me better. Don't you think I would be a good guide?" He walked past her.

Taryn followed him down the row of stables, her reply stuck in her throat. Her stomach was ticking again, completely ignoring her mental pep talk. She took a deep breath. "I just thought you'd have other things to do."

He looked back momentarily, then disappeared into a small room filled with saddles, blankets, bridles, and a jumble of other equipment she couldn't identify. She waited at the doorway, watching him haul a saddle from its peg. "Careful there, hon'," he said, squeezing past her with his load. "Barrel won't be back until the afternoon. I told him I'd take over, so don't worry about my schedule. Maybe we can get to know each other better during the ride."

Taryn tried to will her heartbeat back to a slower, steadier pace.

He disappeared into one of the nearest stalls, hoisting the saddle onto a blanketed horse. The horse's golden coat and blond mane and tail identified it as a palomino. It was a beautiful animal. "This is Ginger. She's for you."

She watched mutely as Douglas ducked into the tack room again. "How long will we be gone?" she finally asked as he threw a saddle onto the black beast. An elegantly hand-painted sign nailed to the stall read SERGEANT.

"As long as you want. A few hours, I expect." He turned to look at her, stepping closer.

Those gray eyes were doing their thing again. Her mind frantically commanded her to look away, but her heart dominated, and her gaze held his.

"Taryn," he asked softly, "you're not afraid of me, are you?"

"No, of course not," she said quickly, frowning. "It's just . . ." She swallowed hard. "It's just . . ." she began again, and faltered. "Oh, never mind." She hated being so flustered. "Let's just go." The conversation with Todd was in the back of her mind, and now Douglas's presence increased the pressure on her frazzled senses. She could feel the energy buzzing between them. Two very different men creating two very different tensions. Todd pushed. Douglas pulled. The push away from Todd's ugliness actually increased the pull toward Douglas's warmth—an abstract and dangerous notion, she admitted. She had to get out of here.

Douglas smiled. "I know."

"You know what?" she asked warily, lowering her eyes. Why wouldn't her feet move? She should back away, but her mind could not make her feet respond.

"It's the attraction thing again, isn't it?" He placed his index finger under her chin, gently lifting her face to return her gaze to his.

She stared into his eyes—her mind mush, her feet apparently rooted to the spot—and opened her mouth to form the word *no,* but no sound came out.

"Your mouth is the perfect shape for kissing when you're about to say no," he whispered, leaning closer and briefly brushing his lips against hers.

Her knees just about added to the other malfunctions her body had suddenly acquired, wobbling for a moment before she willed them straight. The rest of her reactions, however, were not so easy to control. Her entire body tingled from the touch of his lips. Her heart pounded in her chest—surely he could hear it, she thought. Definitely more than just *agreeable;* the words from her conversation with Alison tore through her mind like a brief, comical tempest. And it had to stop, she told herself sternly, managing to take a step back. "We—we can't do anything about this," she stammered, wide-eyed. *Pull yourself together!*

Douglas leaned back against the stall, confident, in total control. "I'm glad you think so. You're right. It's inevitable," he added.

"No! I mean we won't do anything about this—this, ahh, *attraction,* as you call it."

"*Attraction,* as I call it?" His brows raised in amusement. "What would you call it, Taryn?"

She crossed her arms. "This must remain a professional

relationship," she said, hoping he wouldn't hear the desperation that backed her statement.

"That word again," he muttered with distaste. "Why?" he challenged quietly, his stare holding her to the spot.

"Because it's the only way I can do my job."

"Why?" he asked again, obviously curious at her need to separate the two elements. "Don't tell me you can't see any potential here Taryn. Sweetheart, I've seen the wrong often enough to recognize something right when it hits me full in the face."

The words pierced her heart, the shock nearly knocking her over. *Now that,* she admitted with a jolt, *was a little more powerful than casual flirting.* "You don't even know me!"

"I know enough. I know it'd be a crime not to pursue this."

She shook her head slowly. *This isn't what I came here for,* she reminded herself.

"Why does this need to remain a professional relationship?" he prompted again.

"Because business and romance don't mix. I've been there before and I'm not going there again. And I've seen it happen a dozen times, and seen it end in disaster. I can't risk messing this up." *And I'm afraid to give you my heart.* The thought came out of the blue. She had to avert her gaze, looking instead at the palomino's swishing tail in the stall behind him.

"This sounds far too serious."

"I want this job. I need this job. I won't do anything to jeopardize it and I would appreciate it if you would respect that," she finished, moving her gaze back to his, trying to hold her ground.

He continued to stare at her. She felt a heavy warmth uncurl in her abdomen. He shook his head slightly, then stepped forward, eliminating the distance between them. He gently rested his hands on her shoulders, as if he knew she was about to bolt.

As if her feet would let her, she thought sullenly.

"I think you're wrong. First of all, romance has everything to do with people and little to do with the place."

"It's more complicated than that."

"Second, this is not only your place of work, but also your home. There's a difference."

Home? Taryn considered, just for an instant, what it would be like if this beautiful place were her home. Where, exactly, was home? Not with either of her parents. She had no childhood home, had never been in one place long enough. Not her apartment in Vancouver, now surely rented to someone else. A wave of sadness, of rootlessness, pushed against her chest.

". . . but I don't think anything I say will make you see it," Douglas continued. His voice—deep, smooth, and gentle— caressed her frayed nerves, and she tilted her head back slightly to absorb the effect for just a moment. "You'll just have to figure it out for yourself." His thumbs drew little circles on the bare skin of her upper arms, sending thread-thin shivers right down to her toes.

Douglas smiled down into her eyes. "Look, I'm not suggesting a huge commitment right off the bat. Just give it a chance. Taryn, I can hear your heart pounding from here."

Taryn knew she should say something, but the sensations he created were rendering her tongue useless. She closed her eyes, hoping to restore her faculties. "Don't be ridiculous," she murmured with a frown.

He slid his hands slowly up and down her upper arms. Her heart hammered hard and fast against her ribs. Perhaps he could indeed hear it, she admitted absently. She barely managed to stop herself from swaying into him; the events of the past few months had left her desperate for someone to lean on—both physically and emotionally. *Wrong reasons!* her mind shouted.

"We owe it to each other to give it a shot. There's something here, and I know we're going to find it."

She tensed as she tried to re-focus on her priorities.

"Whoa," he said quietly, obviously reading her body language. The soft, smoky glow in his eyes relaxed her slightly, and she exhaled suddenly, realizing that she had forgotten to breathe. "No pressure, Taryn. Maybe you just need to get used to the idea." He took a step away and dropped his hands. "My word, then, that I won't bring it up again today." He gave her a wink. "Unless you do, of course."

She gave herself a mental shake, pulling herself together. "You're far too sure of yourself." She took another breath, self-consciously running her hands up and down her upper arms to tame the goose bumps he'd created. "What, you're hoping I'll throw myself at you? I'm—"

He held up his hand, his expression closing as her words dissipated the tender mood. "Don't say it."

"Don't say what?"

"A professional," he muttered with a slight grimace.

"Why? That's not what I was going to say, but . . . I am," she stated defiantly.

He shook his head, reaching for Ginger's bridle. "You know, you keep tossing that word around—I think it's just a lofty ideal to help justify whatever serves your purpose."

"Now that's a loaded statement if I ever heard one." She grabbed Ginger's reins from him. "I suppose you're going to explain that?"

He hesitated, moving in beside Sergeant, speaking softly to the animal as it tossed its head. Once the bridle was in hand and Sergeant backed out of the stall, he continued, "Let's just say that those who claim to take the moral high road make themselves easy targets." He led Sergeant past her, the horse's big iron-shod feet clomping loudly on the planked floor.

"And just what's that supposed to mean?" Taryn demanded, pulling Ginger into step behind him as they left the stables. "Targets for what?"

They stopped in the sunshine and Douglas began tightening the saddle cinches. She waited impatiently for an explanation. Somewhere in the back of her mind she admitted that anger was so much more comfortable than the more tender feelings prompted by exchange of a few moments ago. Why was that? her conscience prompted. The word *coward* sprang to her mind, but was quickly smothered as Douglas went on.

"They make others want to examine their motives and their actions—examine them, and then question them." He briefly looked her in the eye as he came around to adjust Ginger's saddle.

"Is that so?" She crossed her arms. "Examine what? Question what?"

"You really want to know?"

"You've come this far. Let's have it."

"You took this job. You came here, to a place you know is in trouble, to pad your resume. Well, maybe not *pad* exactly," he retracted at her look of shock. "But you make no secret of the fact that you're using your short contract here as nothing more than a stepping stone to a better job back in Vancouver." He grunted on the last word as he heaved on Ginger's cinch.

"I've been honest about that from the start. It doesn't mean I won't do a good job."

"I realize that. But a true professional—since you constantly remind me that you are one—would consider each contract as the 'be all and end all' of her career. Or," he smiled slightly as he continued, "at least give her employer that impression."

"But that's lying."

"No, it's only lying if someone asks you the question and you answer it dishonestly. Coming to a new job—especially if you know the place is struggling and not many others would touch it with a ten foot pole—and giving the impression that there's no other place you'd rather be working . . . now that's professionalism." He paused, glancing at Taryn's legs, then to

Ginger's saddle stirrups. Seemingly satisfied with the stirrups' length, he gave them a final tug and walked back to Sergeant.

"You've mentioned the Stanley Park Hotel and how Aiden will be here in September and how he might make you a job offer. How do you think that makes people here feel?"

He swung into the saddle with ease, indicating that she should do the same. She did, albeit rather awkwardly.

"Your stirrups okay?"

She pushed her heels down, not quite able to fully straighten her legs. "Fine, I think," she murmured absently, wanting to return to the subject at hand. "But what about—"

"Hold on. I know what you're going to say. It's a short contract, right? That's not the point, but it leads to another." He nudged Sergeant into a walk. Ginger followed automatically, without a signal from Taryn.

"Pray, do tell," Taryn remarked sarcastically.

"A true professional would look for ways to help the inn for the future, whether or not that meant a contract extension." He leaned over and pushed open the corral gate. It swung on well-greased hinges, barely making a sound. He rode through, and held the gate for Taryn and Ginger.

"That's not fair," Taryn protested, trying to keep her voice even. "And an unreasonable expectation. Besides, I haven't been here long enough to get into that." She shifted her seat, trying to get accustomed to the saddle and the rocking motion of Ginger's gait.

"Who said anything about fair? I'm just showing you what happens when you keep spouting off about how professional you are, or claim to be. It makes you an easy target for criticism."

She waited as he manoeuvred Sergeant into position to close the corral gate. Is that what it looked like—like she didn't want to be here? Although she felt very defensive about his words right now, she tried to put herself in his shoes. It burned to admit he had a point.

"I'm sorry if my enthusiasm about Aiden was misinterpreted," she offered. "I can't help but be excited about the prospect. But that's about all I'm going to apologize for. I'm here to do my very, very best for the inn. The fact that it's also in my interest to do so is nothing I need to be sorry for."

"I'm not asking you to apologize." He and Sergeant took the lead again. "I'm just getting tired of hearing that word so I thought I'd let you know how it can come across."

"You know, most of time I mention it because of something you're doing, or suggesting."

"Ahh, that's another story." He turned briefly and grinned. "You use it to cramp my style."

She almost smiled in spite of herself, but covered it with an unladylike groan. "Are you done then?"

"Well, there is a corollary to all of that."

She couldn't see his face, but sensed his smile. "Oh please, don't stop now then," she invited sweetly.

"Since you asked . . ." he paused a moment and looked back at her, seeming to search for the right words. He slowed Sergeant until the horses were abreast. "From where I'm sitting, you let that word—*professional*—rule your life. Not just your work, but your life. You use it like some kind of, well, I guess like some kind of armor, something you throw on whenever you feel something you're uncomfortable with."

"What?" Taryn sputtered. "How could you say such a terrible thing?"

"Well, I'm done now."

"You certainly are." She stared at him as the words sank in, then pulled her gaze away and concentrated on Ginger's gait for a few moments.

"That's a rather personal attack, don't you think?" she said finally. As much as she'd always prided herself in being able to accept constructive criticism, she felt physically and emotionally injured. Maybe it was because the words came from Douglas. His good opinion had become increasingly important to her. Or maybe it was because she felt she'd taken enough of a beating in the past couple of months. Her experience at the inn was supposed to be a new start. She sighed. "I use it—if you want to look at it that way—to help me face challenges in an efficient, effective way."

He stopped Sergeant. Ginger stopped too. Taryn briefly wondered why she had the reins in her hand at all, since the animal just mimicked Sergeant's movements.

"Sometimes, I guess, but that's not always how I see it, Taryn. It's an interesting trait of yours, and I find myself wondering why. Look," he began leaning over to better see her face, which she kept expressionless as she focused on re-wrapping her reins around her hand. "Don't wrap them, Taryn. If you get thrown, you'll get dragged." He paused when she wouldn't look at him. "Sweetheart, I don't know how this all got started. Forget it."

She lanced him and sighed.

He gave her a conciliatory grin, then added, "Of course, a true professional would take this all in stride."

She threw her notepad at him as he nudged Sergeant ahead. He caught it deftly, laughing, then briefly reined up again to hand it back to her. "I just wanted you to see what it looks like from this side. Forget it. We're lucky to have you."

Douglas gave a sharp whistle, causing Chip to come bounding up out of nowhere, then urged Sergeant into an easy trot. Ginger followed. The new pace negated any need for Taryn to reply. She clung to the saddle horn and tried to keep from bouncing. For the moment the distraction was welcome. Whether she wanted to or not, she'd be thinking about his words in the days and weeks to come. They'd join the other concerns on her mental back burner. Right now she had a trail ride and some marketing research to complete. She bit her lip and held on as Ginger followed Sergeant through a little creek and up the first rise.

But how long, she wondered, before those back burner pots of hers would boil over?

Chapter Six

He *must have known I don't ride much,* Taryn thought with gratitude as Ginger plodded obediently behind Sergeant. If Ginger had stomped and fussed as much as Sergeant had on their climb into the benchlands, she would have found herself in the sagebrush a few times already. It hadn't seemed to bother Douglas any, she thought, admiring his strong back and the way he held his seat.

Taryn turned to look at the valley spread out to their left. It was a perfect view, the lake below was framed between two solitary and ancient ponderosa pines just down the slope. She loosely wrapped her reins around the saddle horn and pulled her camera out of her pouch, not bothering to stop Ginger. The palomino was moving slowly enough for Taryn to take a clear photo.

Her finger squeezed the shutter button when Douglas's voice rang out sharply. "Never drop your reins, Taryn. You're just asking for trouble."

Taryn released the shutter and lowered the camera to look at him, ready to point out that Ginger couldn't make a fast move if her life depended on it. Suddenly a grouse shot out from a juniper bush to their right with Chip in hot pursuit, startling Ginger into a quick side-step and a dash toward

Sergeant. Taryn grabbed the saddle horn with her free hand, her feet coming out of the stir-ups as her body was thrown backward and sideways. It was only a few fast steps, and Ginger came to an abrupt halt as Douglas gripped her bridle, but not before Taryn slid out of the saddle. She landed in a heap in the dust beside Ginger, camera held up out of harm's way.

Douglas was out of his saddle and at her side in a split second. "Bloody hell," he said, gripping her elbow and helping her to her feet. The concern in his voice was as pronounced as the frown on his face.

"I'm fine." Taryn felt the flush of embarrassment sting her cheeks as she dusted herself off. "Not one of my more graceful moves, I'll admit."

Relief was evident as he smiled back. "I'd forgotten how accident-prone you are."

"Very funny," she snapped.

"Sharp tongue too," Douglas remarked, helping her dust off the back of her jeans.

"I can manage, thanks." She removed his hand, then dropped it as though it were on fire. Was every physical contact going to have this effect on her? Her thoughts kept wandering back to their conversation in the barn. Part of her continued to whisper "coward," while another part kept repeating "stay the course." He'd really shaken her with his words, his invitation to—to what, exactly? A relationship, a courtship? Did it matter, in any case? She'd already decided not to risk her job, or her heart.

"Just trying to help." He shrugged. "I'd guessed you hadn't ridden much."

"City girl," she replied, straightening her baseball cap and turning to mount Ginger again. She felt his strong hands on her hips, assisting her into the saddle as though she weighed nothing. She turned to look at him, trying to gauge if he meant the interaction to be as personal as it felt to her, or whether it stemmed from simple concern for her safety.

He looked innocent, or, she thought discouragingly, as innocent as a black-haired personification of temptation could possibly look. She turned away, struggling to return her camera to her pack and finally hanging the strap around her neck instead. She reminded herself of what had possessed her to venture into this backcountry with him. "Let's go," she said firmly, driving her thoughts away from his hands to her original purpose. "I need to get some material for this ad and get back to the inn before lunch."

The bunchgrass and sagebrush disappeared as they left the valley floor, and was gradually replaced by Ponderosa pine and the sprawling juniper bushes, with their blue-gray berries, just coming into color this late in the summer. As they continued to climb, the forest thickened, and Taryn recognized an abundance of Douglas fir, thinking immediately of its reputation as the perfect Christmas tree. She briefly envisioned Douglas stomping about in the snow to cut one for his living room. What a change from hauling one home in the rain from the corner gas station, like she did in Vancouver last year. Her stomach gave an odd twist at the memory.

"Are those birch?" Taryn pointed to a large stand in a deep ravine sloping slightly to their left.

Douglas turned slightly to follow her gaze. "Mostly aspen and alder." He paused. "You're right, there's some birch in there as well. Do you know how to tell?"

"Not really," she confessed. "It was a guess."

He slowed Sergeant until they were abreast. "The aspen bark is smooth, white or the palest of green, and has black scars where old branches once grew. Its leaves quiver with the slightest breeze, sometimes making the tree look like it's shimmering. They do that because the leaf stalks are flatter than most, and only allow the leaf blade to turn from side to side. The local natives call the tree "women's tongues" in their own language."

"And why is that?" Taryn ventured.

"Because they don't seem to stop moving." He said it with a straight face, but Taryn saw a twinkle in his eye.

She eyed him sceptically.

"It's true. Ask Tina or Susan when you get back to the inn. Anyway," he began pulling ahead momentarily as a fallen log narrowed their path. When they were abreast again he continued. "The birch is easy to identify because its bark is always peeling—good fire-starter, that papery stuff. It's usually white, or reddish brown where it's just been peeled, with dark horizontal slits as scars. And its leaves are toothed."

"And the natives?"

"I'm not sure what they called it. But I think I remember Gordon saying that they drank the sap to cure colds."

Taryn cringed.

"I've wondered if that works, but never had the nerve to try it," he laughed. "And then there's the alder. It's much smaller than the birch or aspen, and grows in clumps, more often like a huge shrub than a single tree. Its leaves are toothed like the birch, but slightly more oval-shaped. It's the bark that's the give-away. It's grayish-brown, and its scars are pale and oval, not dark slits like the others. The natives use alder wood to smoke their fish and meat because it doesn't flavor the food."

Taryn was impressed. "You should be doing some nature walks for our guests."

He shook his head. "Gordon was my teacher. He should be doing the walks. He's a natural."

"It's a great idea." Taryn made a mental note of it, reining up slightly to let Douglas ride ahead as the trail narrowed again. The air had warmed considerably since they first set out, and if not for the constant breeze cooling her skin, the heat would have been oppressive. She'd worn bike shorts under her jeans, just in case it got too hot, but soon realized that long pants were essential to protect her legs from protruding branches and saddle chafing. Chip returned, panting furiously, tongue hanging, and resumed his sentinel duties beside Sergeant.

The forest floor lay tinder-dry, the horses' hooves rustled through crisp pine needles, snapping small twigs and crunching pinecones already discarded by the trees. The wind, the creaking of her leather saddle, and the occasional snort as Ginger or Sergeant blew dust out of their nostrils were the only other sounds.

After a few minutes, Douglas turned and pointed up the trail. "This heads around the back of the hill and onto the plateau where there's an old miner's shack, much like the one where you and Chip first met," he added with a chuckle. She gave him a wrinkly-nosed grimace. "From up there you can get a great shot of the whole valley—lake, golf course, inn, ranch buildings. Are you game?"

"Perfect," she nodded.

He nudged Sergeant into a walk. "From there, we'll take a different trail back. Follow the creek. It flows into Aspen Falls, and then curves back around, leading to the inn from the other side."

"A waterfall?" She was impressed and curious, giving Ginger a little kick to move up alongside him, both surprised and proud when the animal responded. "I didn't know anything about a waterfall."

"It's not a big one, only about twenty feet high. There isn't too much run-off now, not like in the spring, but it's cool and fresh. A great place to picnic and go for a quick swim."

"Great selling point." Taryn was impressed. "Accessible only on horseback?"

"Pretty much. There's a rough gravel road from the inn to my cabin, and a path leading from there to the falls, but that's not a public access."

"Even better." She smiled at him, enthused at this discovery. The mention of his cabin was intriguing too, and she wondered if she would be able to see it from the trail.

It was uncomfortably warm now, and Taryn dug into her pouch for her water bottle.

"You're easy to please," Douglas remarked casually.

"I beg your pardon?" Taryn wiped her mouth with the back of her hand and returned the bottle to her bag.

"Your face just lights up whenever I tell you something about the ranch or the inn. You're easy to please." He looked over at her and smiled.

She shrugged. "You're telling me good things. Good, marketable things. It makes my job easier."

"Well, for what it's worth, with your efforts I think the inn will finish the season off in reasonably good shape. I just hope it'll be enough to keep the creditors off our backs for another year."

Taryn wondered if this was an effort to smooth over his earlier criticisms of her professionalism. Those remarks still burned. If she were due an apology, then this might be as good as it got. For the sake of a peaceful and productive working relationship, she decided to see it as such. "I appreciate your confidence," Taryn said, returning his smile.

Their horses labored up the slope. Eventually they reached a wide plateau dotted with bunchgrass and other squat, tufted growth. It spread ahead and to their left, and seemed to drop off into the lake far below. To their right, the highest peaks were craggy rock faces, with the occasional shrub or stunted pine clinging precariously to a crevice.

Taryn raised her face to a brief, cool breeze, then nudged Ginger forward to follow Douglas toward a weathered shack near the edge of the plateau. She moved her toes in her boots, trying to keep her legs from falling asleep.

"Legs that feel this sore couldn't be asleep," she assured herself with a whisper. Her rear end ached too, and she wiggled in her saddle, trying to get the blood circulating in that area again. Her pains were forgotten once she caught up to Douglas, who had reined up beside the shack.

He hadn't exaggerated. The view was spectacular. The

lake mirrored the clear blue sky. The vivid, irrigated green of the golf course glowed like an emerald on the lake's far side, a stark contrast to the rougher, sun-bleached ground around it. From this distance, Taryn could barely make out a few people moving on the beach area, and in the gardens behind the inn. The inn itself looked like a Victorian dollhouse. On the near side of the lake, a dozen or so horses moved around in the corral. The ranch buildings huddled around the big red barn. An idyllic setting, a picture-perfect home, Taryn thought wistfully, guessing it was what Douglas saw with pride when he looked at it.

Home. He'd said this was now her home too. Perhaps it was, if temporary residence counted. She'd had many then, in her life, but none of them held any particular home-like memories. Certainly not in the way this view must for him. She took off her cap and ran her fingers through her hair, letting the cool breeze toss it about for a moment. She stared at the view and wondered what it would really take to make a place feel like home, in that perfect, greeting-card way. Comfort and security, she supposed. And acceptance . . . and love. It was a guess. And work—something constructive to do, surely? *You're really not certain, are you?* She settled her cap back in place and pushed the musings away.

Taryn spent the next twenty minutes shooting photos. She captured the shack in some, Douglas and Chip in others, genuinely pleased at the site he had chosen.

"All done," she said, slipping her camera back into the pouch and preparing to mount Ginger.

"Did you see the bear?"

"The what?" Taryn looked around quickly.

"The bear. A black bear." He turned and pointed out over the lake. "It's over there, on the other side, about halfway up the slope."

Relieved that the bear was not nearby, Taryn left Ginger and went to stand beside him, searching the hills opposite them. "Where? I can't see it."

"Come here then." He put an arm around her, steering her to stand directly in front of him. She could feel the heat of his solid chest against her back, feel the size of him as he laid his arm across her shoulder, his chin brushing the top of her cap. He pressed her head against the soft denim covering his powerful bicep so she could look down the length of his arm to see where he was pointing. The intimacy of the position was unnerving, and her heart skipped a beat before starting to pound in earnest. She tried to concentrate. He smelled wonderful—of earth and forest and leather, with the hint of sandalwood she remembered from their first meeting.

Home.

"Right there, just below the patch of trees, in a direct line up from the pro shop," Douglas directed quietly, his head bent beside hers, his breath warm on her ear as he spoke. "See him now? He's after the Saskatoon berries that grow up there."

"Wow! He looks big even from here!" Taryn remarked, hoping Douglas would interpret her breathlessness as excitement about seeing the bear instead of the spell he was creating by his embrace.

Douglas drew his hand back, resting it casually on her shoulder. "He's not that big really, not like a grizzly, but I still wouldn't want to get on his bad side."

They stood watching the bear a few moments longer, until it lumbered up the slope and disappeared into the trees. The feel of his hand on her shoulder was a friendly gesture, Taryn told herself, but his touch suffused her flesh with a tingling sensation that left her slightly light-headed. She berated herself for her reaction. If she could get accustomed to his casual contact, life would be much easier.

Taryn stiffened as Douglas turned her around to face him, resting his hands on her shoulders.

"What?" she asked, dropping her eyes and pretending to fuss with her camera.

He sighed audibly, brushing his knuckles against her cheek, then dropped his hands. "Nothing."

Taryn closed her eyes, knowing that if she looked at him now, his gaze would pull her into a kiss—one that her heart was telling her would be heavenly. The protests of her head were slowly being drowned out by the wind, the sun, the landscape, and . . . this man. How was she ever going to get through this day with her sanity intact? Even now she could feel herself drawn toward him like a magnet. "We should be going," she said quickly, turning to Ginger.

The sun burned hot, and at this point their trail through a sparse forest offered only intermittent shade. The dust was beginning to stick to her skin now, her sunblock's moisture and her own perspiration providing just the right adhesive. By the end of the ride she was certain she would look like a trail-weary tomboy.

They rode on in easy silence for some time, eventually beginning a gradual descent and meeting the creek. Taryn was increasingly absorbed in the tranquil beauty of their surroundings. The trees grew slightly larger now, and the grass, shrubs, and other undergrowth became more abundant as they continued down slope. The temperature dropped slightly too, as shade began to dominate their path, with only occasional sunny patches to illuminate the puffs of dust kicked up by the horses. The giggle of water flowing over a rocky creek bed accompanied them on their left, while overhead tiny sparrows flitted from branch to branch, chirping at the intrusion.

Peace, Taryn thought with a sigh. From a business perspective, it was exactly what stressed urbanites needed for a break. From a personal perspective, it was exactly what she needed too. Saddle sores and a few unsettling moments with Douglas aside, she felt more content at this moment than . . . well, she reflected, since when? She couldn't remember.

The creek gradually became wider and deeper, its giggling growing throatier until it bore the sound of serious rushing water. The air was fresher too, she noticed; not as dry and dusty. She inhaled deeply.

"Are we there?" she called out eagerly, not even trying to

hide her enthusiasm. She gave Ginger a little kick, nudging her closer to where Douglas had stopped at what turned out to be the edge of an escarpment. He turned in his saddle as she approached, catching the enthusiasm in her voice and returning her smile with a grin of his own.

"Have I ever mentioned that you're easy to please?" he remarked again as Ginger came to a stop beside Sergeant. Taryn said nothing, searching his face for a hint of mockery. She found none. Only the soft gray eyes and the easy smile that warmed her heart. He also looked relaxed, Taryn thought. There certainly was something timeless and thera-peutic about the forest. It was as if the rest of the world didn't exist.

"We can lead the horses down the side trail over there," he indicated with nod of his head. "It's a bit rough, but not dan-gerous. It'll take us down to the bottom where the pool is. You should get some good photos there."

Douglas stepped around to Ginger's left side and grabbed Taryn firmly by the hips as she came off the horse. His touch lingered just a second longer than necessary as he set her on the ground against his body. Her legs ached but she rallied valiantly, managing at least the appearance of stability.

Leading the horses, they picked their way down the small path, into the thickest vegetation they'd yet encountered on their outing. The relatively abundant moisture provided by the creek and the falls had created a new micro-climate. Alders, aspens, birch, cottonwoods—and a few others Taryn couldn't identify—had all made their homes here. Tall grasses and clumps of choke cherries, prickly gooseberries, and wild roses filled in as undergrowth.

With horses in tow and Chip trail-blazing ahead, they ducked and dodged their way into what Taryn immediately termed Aspen Valley's Little Garden of Eden. She was stunned at the unexpected beauty of the place, looking around in wonder as Douglas led both horses to a smaller side pool where they could drink and rest. For the next few minutes Taryn had her camera clicking off shots as she explored the site through the viewfinder. She caught Douglas in a few of her frames, his strong hands tending to the horses, the falls behind him.

He fits in here. Perfectly.

The falls were not much higher than twenty feet, as Douglas had mentioned. They didn't carry enough water to be described as thundering, but they poured over the edge of the escarpment in a steady flow about four or five feet wide, splashing freely into a boulder-strewn pool. A number of other large boulders edged the pool, forming ideal theater seats for the waterfalls' symphony of sound and movement.

Taryn stared at the water cascading from above, spellbound by the simple beauty of it. Suddenly the heat, trail dust, and the pangs of loneliness and rootlessness that had been growing inside her since her arrival at Aspen Creek all collided into a great desire to plunge into the pool. Clothes and all, if need be. She needed to just stand under the falls and let the water clear her head and her heart.

"Are you going to stand there staring, or are you going in?" Douglas asked.

She looked at him, her mind racing with sudden questions she didn't want to ask, let alone answer. Would her efforts for the inn be enough? Would the inn survive? Was Douglas really interested in her, or was she just a game, a conquest? And why did that matter? Did she belong here? Where was home? Would Todd really follow through on his threats? Was her career on the rocks? Where was all of this coming from? Her back burner pots were boiling over and about to catch fire. Tears welled in her eyes to extinguish them.

She pressed her fingertips to her temples, bit her lip, and swallowed hard, looking back at the falls in an effort to stop the deluge of thoughts and emotions.

"Taryn?"

She heard the concern in Douglas's voice and mentally shook herself free from the introspection. "It's absolutely beautiful. Do you swim in it?" She turned to him, managing a weak smile.

"It's not very deep, about up to my chest, and yes, I swim in it. My cabin's just up there," he pointed to the other side of the falls, "so I spend a bit of time here."

Taryn looked in the direction he had pointed, thankful that her eyes were once again dry. Up on the ridge, through the trees, she could barely make out an attractive—and large— log cabin with a peaked roof and a covered porch. She strained her neck, but was unable to see more. "You call that a cabin? Aren't cabins supposed to be small, rickety, one-room things? It looks more like a house to me, and a rather large one at that."

He shrugged, looking up at it. "It's home."

"Looks gorgeous." Taryn was impressed. It looked new too, and she wondered if he'd had it built when he got engaged, with plans to raise his family there. She couldn't ask, though. She glanced at him, then back at the house. Yes, it certainly suited him. She pictured him relaxing by the fire, stretched out on an oversized sofa. She wondered what made it home for him. Was it just a place to live, or more than that?

Taryn did a double take, turning to look at him again, this time in alarm. "What do you think you're doing?"

"I'm going in," he said matter-of-factly, pulling his shirt free.

"You brought your swimsuit?" She averted her eyes, looking back at the pool instead, the cool, clear water splashing in from the rocks above. Why hadn't he told her before they left? Would she have brought her swimsuit? Probably not. At that time she would not have even considered swimming with him. It just seemed too . . . well . . . personal. But after two hours of heat, trail dust, and aching muscles, however, the idea had some merit.

"No, I didn't."

Each undone button revealed another two inches of his muscled chest, tanned and roughened with dark, coarse hair.

"So, what are you doing?" she all but croaked, realization hitting her like a truck. The man was taking his clothes off!

He looked up at her, tossing his shirt onto a rock. "I'm going in. Aren't you?"

As his fingers grasped the buttoned fly of his jeans, Taryn turned quickly, stepping onto one of the boulders forming the edge of the pool. She pretended to be enthralled by the waterfall itself, which would not be too far from the truth if Cowboy Man hadn't been creating an advertising idea a garment company would die for. She had never thought of herself as a prude, but this man's boldness was simply overwhelming.

"I didn't bring anything appropriate to wear," she remarked, surprised at how priggish that sounded. She could swim in her shorts, of course, and she wore a sports bra and tank top under her long-sleeved shirt. Nothing wrong with that. Squatting down to run her hand through the water, she sighed in spite of herself at its cool freshness.

"Appropriate is a relative term, don't you think?"

Taryn heard him enter the water, turning to notice with relief he'd left his boxers on. "Well, thank heaven for small mercies," she murmured. He turned when he was immersed to his chest, looking at her with a grin. She wondered if he knew he looked like some kind of mythical water god.

"Don't be shy. 'When in Rome, do as the Romans do.' " He immersed himself completely then, thrusting up out of the water with his hands pushing his gleaming black hair out of his face, muscles glistening, water dripping from every hard curve. "You have no idea how good this feels. C'mon," he tossed his head back in a beckoning gesture, "I gave you my word, remember? And if you're worried about your *professional* image," he stressed the word with a hint of disdain, "be assured that what happens here won't leave here." He pelted a stream of water at her with the flat of his hand, sending a cool spray onto her bare arm.

Taryn stared at him, feeling hot, sticky, and dirty. He turned, moving away from her, toward the falls. He held out his hands, letting the water splash over them, then moved his whole body under the flow. The beauty of it, the way he connected with one of earth's most basic elements in such a natural and sensual way, was breathtaking.

Something inside her suddenly gave way. What was she waiting for? For once in her life she was going to throw caution to the wind and indulge. What she wanted to feel right now was that cool, clear water enveloping her body on this gorgeous day, with this gorgeous man, in this gorgeous and mystical place in the middle of nowhere. She needed a catharsis, and this was it.

Oh, don't be so dramatic. It's just a swim, for heaven's sake! It wasn't too personal or unprofessional. It was just a swim.

Douglas turned just as she was struggling to remove her boots and swam the few strokes it took to reach her boulder. "So you've succumbed to the seductive power of the pool, have you?" he teased.

Taryn couldn't make herself meet his eyes after that comment. "Don't get your hopes up," she said with a smile. "I'm wearing shorts under my jeans."

"Me? Hopes up?" he responded with mock injury as he turned back to the falls. "You'd think after what we've been through so far—"

"Oh, shut up."

"Again with that sharp tongue," he admonished over his shoulder. "And for such a pretty lady."

"Humph." She whipped off her cap and stood to peel off her jeans. The blouse came off next, and she dropped it next to her jeans, then slid into the water. The cold shock stole her breath. She dunked her head right away, revelling in the icy bliss.

When she came up for air he was smiling at her again. "Feel great?"

She nodded and returned the smile, moving toward the falls.

They stood about three feet apart, letting the cold, fresh water pound over them like a massage. After a moment, Taryn stepped out of the flow, pushing the hair out of her eyes. She watched him as he stood, eyes closed, hands clasped behind his neck, water pummelling his tanned, muscled body. He was truly the most beautiful man she had ever met. Right now she was too far away, both mentally and physically, from all the rules and logic in her life not to be able to admit, at least to herself, that she was in real danger of falling in love. The admission shocked her.

But she was not so far removed from reality that she was going to let it happen.

Douglas opened his eyes to look at her just then. Taryn didn't know if he could even see her for all the water hitting him. But then he stepped out of the falls and locked his gaze with hers. She moved as if entranced when he took her hand and led her away from the spray.

He stopped and turned to face her, hands gently resting on her shoulders, the gray of his eyes searching hers intensely. "I'm going to kiss you. If you don't want that, you'd better say so now."

She couldn't even look away, let alone protest. He didn't give her any more time to think about it, lowering his lips to hers.

The kiss was short. Too short. She opened her eyes as he separated his lips from hers, her breathing unsteady. She wondered why she had let it happen, at the same time knowing she had never felt so alive in all her life.

"What are you doing to me?" he whispered with a warm smile as he lowered his lips again. His fingers linked with hers under the water.

She closed her eyes. *Steady.*

Nothing.

Her eyes flew open. His face was farther away now. He was shaking his head, looking pained. "I'm sorry. I shouldn't have done that. I gave you my word that this wouldn't happen today." He unlinked their hands, then ran his through his thick wet hair with a small groan. "You just looked so perfectly kissable at that moment." He smiled again and shrugged.

Embarrassment flooded her cheeks. She'd wanted that next kiss. Asked for it with everything but words. He'd turned her down, point blank. She felt cheap, insulted. She'd been unfairly tested, and had failed miserably. She opened her mouth to speak, to admonish him for manipulating her, but before any sound came out he leaned back, taking first her hands and then wrapping his arms around her, submerging them both into the cold water.

"Let me go!" she sputtered as they came up, violently pushing away from him. She couldn't get out of the pool fast enough, the water's resistance adding to her frustration as she headed toward the boulder where she'd left her clothes. It was a game for him, after all. He'd toyed with her, proved his charm.

"Taryn, it wasn't supposed to happen like this."

Taryn struggled to pull her jeans on over her wet shorts. It was a disgusting feeling, adding to her foul temper, made worse as the dampness seeped into her jeans and blouse. She was overreacting, she knew. It wasn't such a big deal. It shouldn't be such a big deal. But, dammit, she just wanted to get out of there and away from him.

Douglas caught her by the shoulders as she was about to mount Ginger. He turned her toward him. "That was unplanned."

She gritted her teeth and looked away. "Sure. Fine. Forget it."

"Never in a million years," he said quietly, then smiled knowingly. "If I hadn't given you my word, you'd be raising your lips to mine again right now, and I'd be in heaven."

His teasing was more than she could bear. Her palm connected with his cheek before she knew what she'd done. The crack of flesh against flesh seemed to still the sounds of the water and forest around them.

Taryn was instantly sorry. His hand grasped her wrist like an iron clamp, slowly lowering it back to her side. His lips and jaw drew tight. A small red splotch appeared on his cheek, and she stared at it, and then at his big hand immobilizing hers. Panic clogged her throat as memories flooded back—memories of a cramped two-seater car, Todd's strong hand clamped on her wrist, trying to prevent her from leaving. She wrenched her hand, trying to free it.

Douglas released his grip immediately and she staggered back. He caught her shoulders, more gently this time, but firmly held her in place to face him. "Should we get into a debate on whether or not I deserved that?" He looked more bewildered than angry.

"No. I'm sorry." What on earth was wrong with her? Could she not get a grip on herself? She turned away from him and mounted Ginger, wishing she could disappear, more ashamed at her behavior now than before.

Chapter Seven

Hours later and bone weary, Taryn limped up the last few steps to the quiet solitude of the inn's top floor. It had been a long and busy day. Her leg muscles ached terribly from the morning's adventure, as did her heart and her dignity. She hadn't seen Douglas since their tense, silent parting at the stables at noon, and for that she was thankful.

The bathroom door stood ajar; the night light above the sink bathed the room in a pale glow. The white claw-foot tub called to her, its chiffon shower curtain billowing in the breeze from the open window.

Within minutes she was up to her chin in steaming water and a swollen cloud of magnolia-scented bubbles that threatened to spill over the sides of the tub. The night light was her candle. She sat gazing at the stars in the black night sky, feeling the breeze caress her face as the hot water soothed her aching body and calmed her soul.

Taryn closed her eyes and sighed, leaning her head back against the towel she had rolled up as a pillow on the tub's edge. Paradise found.

Footsteps sounded on the stairs. She strained her ears. No, it couldn't be Gertrude and Hans. They never came up the stairs quietly. And they didn't wear boots. That would leave . . . him. She sank down lower into the tub, the desire to hide over-riding the logic that he could not possibly know she was there.

She heard him go into his room, then footsteps in the hall again, coming toward the bathroom. *Oh great, he's wants in here.* Thank goodness she had locked the door.

"Occupied, I'm afraid," she called as he tried the door. "I'll just be a few more minutes." She didn't know if she could actually haul herself out of the tub within the next half hour, but it just seemed like the thing to say. Perhaps he'd have the good sense to use one of the guest bathrooms downstairs.

"I just need to wash up and shave," he called quietly through the door. "I'll only be a few minutes too."

She frowned. What did that mean? Was she supposed to let him in and resume her bath later? His sigh, audible through the door, was followed by footsteps back to his room.

She closed her eyes again, letting her muscles turn to jelly.

A few minutes later he was back. He rapped softly on the door. "How are you doing in there?"

"A few more minutes please. Can't you go downstairs?"

"There are teenaged girls in all three guest bathrooms downstairs. I don't have the energy for that."

She smiled, remembering the three families that had arrived during the afternoon, each with a pair of teenaged girls. "A gentleman wouldn't rush a lady through her bath." She knew she was being selfish, but she just couldn't bring herself to move.

"Have I ever been anything less than a gentleman with you?"

"Right now comes to mind," she said pointedly.

"Especially now. I know you're in there in blissful darkness. I could hit the overhead light and glare you out. Worse, I could get the key."

She sat up at that. "You wouldn't dare."

"Depends on how long you take and how tired I get."

She sighed and pulled herself up. Negotiating through a bathroom door was hardly conducive to relaxation anyway, so she may as well just finish up. "Okay, okay. Hold on. I'm done." She quickly washed up, dried off, and wrapped herself in her robe. She switched on one of the lamps above the mirror, filling the room with a soft light so that she could collect her things.

"Happy?" she remarked in mock exasperation as she opened the door.

He pushed himself away from the wall and entered, stepping right to the sink. "Thank you. I thought I was going to fall asleep out there."

She rolled her eyes, pushing her feet into her slippers. "I wasn't that long, for heaven's sake."

His reflection showed the dark stubble shadowing his handsome face as he ran his hand over it. He did, indeed, look exhausted. Their eyes met in the mirror and held for a moment before he bent toward his shaving implements.

"Think of it as a man's way of getting the bathroom to himself," he said with a small smile as he began applying shaving cream.

"Hmmph." Taryn crouched to retrieve her socks from under the chair. She couldn't help but wince, and a small groan escaped as she straightened, her leg muscles protesting the movement.

He didn't miss that. "Sore from riding?" he asked casually, lathering his face.

"Just a bit." A massive understatement.

"You'll really be suffering tomorrow if you don't put something on those muscles."

"I'm sure I'll be fine, thanks for your concern. A longer soak in the tub might have helped," she added caustically.

He ignored that. "I know you hate to admit I'm right,

but it's the truth. It'll be ten times worse tomorrow," he warned as he stroked the razor along his jaw line, the soft scraping sound of blade against stubble reaching her ears. It seemed such an intimate activity to witness. She felt herself blush.

"Why don't you go to your room and do whatever you need to do, and I'll be there in a minute with some ointment. A special cowboy blend—works like magic. I can even put it on for you," he offered innocently.

She didn't miss the twinkle in his eye. He was baiting her again. "You can't be serious."

"I wouldn't offer if I wasn't serious." He kept his attention focused on the mirror, inching the blade along that strong jaw.

"I think not," she said, turning to leave.

"You'll be sorry tomorrow. Don't say I didn't warn you."

She stepped through the doorway and tried not to limp down the hall, then stopped. Was this like cutting off her nose to spite her face? It wouldn't hurt just to have him *bring* the ointment. At this point, she wasn't even certain she would be able to sleep tonight without taking some pain killers, much less walk tomorrow.

She turned back toward the bathroom, watching his hand move the blade along his cheek. "Maybe you could just bring some by," she ventured.

"I'll be there in a minute," he replied without even looking at her.

The night was warm. After dressing in shorts and a t-shirt, Taryn propped her bedroom door open with a chair, a pre-bedtime ritual that created a steady, cooling draft between the open windows in her bedroom and those in the hallway. Moments later she sat rubbing a heady, pine-scented ointment into her calves. The ointment's cooling sensation was amplified by the strong breeze. She had to admit it felt rather good.

"Are you sure this stuff works?" she asked, re-dipping her fingers into the jar Douglas held out for her.

"Positive," he stated firmly. "But your method of application leaves a lot to be desired."

She stopped briefly to scowl at him, then continued her ministrations. "I'm doing just fine, thank you. You don't need to stay. I can manage."

"It's not like putting on suntan lotion, Taryn. Here, like this." In one smooth motion he kneeled before her, applied the gooey gel to his hands and reached for her leg.

Words of protest formed on her lips, but were replaced by a tiny groan of pleasure as his strong fingers began kneading her calf like a practised masseur's.

"Better?" he asked, switching to the other leg.

She let him take it, leaning back into her chair.

And from what part of your professional handbook is this? She tried to concentrate on how to ask him to stop, but the words wouldn't come. It felt glorious.

She heard him expel a long sigh as his hands slowed to a stop. "I think you can probably take it from here."

"Right. Thanks. Yes." She took the jar from him as he perched himself on the chair that held the door. Keeping her head down, confused by the air of expectation building between them, she tried to concentrate on rubbing the ointment into her muscles, knowing he watched her every move.

I could fall in love with this man. The idea and the warmth it generated emanated from deep inside, flowed into her limbs—and then ran smack into a wall of paralyzing fear. She stilled her hands, closed her eyes and took a deep breath.

"Taryn?"

A storm of thoughts suddenly whirled through her mind—her life and career expectations, her mother's warnings, her own needs, principles, the Hagen fiasco, the morning's disaster . . . They collided with each other and crashed into the beauty of what could be . . . and then they smothered it. She wanted to cry in frustration.

She shook her head, opening her eyes, afraid of what she'd see.

He was still for a moment, then released a long, loud sigh. "Okay Taryn." He paused again, then ran both hands through his hair, obviously exasperated, though he kept it from his voice. "Remember what we talked about this morning, in the barn? Taryn, look at me."

"The bit about professionalism?"

"That, and the bit about the potential here, between us."

She nodded.

"So what's wrong?"

She shook her head. "Lots, when it comes to this."

"You don't feel safe."

That was an odd way to put it, but after a moment she realized it was true. That just about summed it up. "No, I don't."

"Part of what I was trying to say this morning was that you seem to use your professionalism to give you emotional distance. Distance makes you feel safe."

Interesting analysis. "Maybe."

"But you obviously don't feel safe. And since you haven't discarded your professionalism, I would guess that there's something else making you keep your emotional distance." He paused, then dragged his chair closer to hers. He took her hand. She let him. His hand enveloped hers with a soothing strength. They sat very still and silent that way for a moment or two.

"You're not afraid of me."

His hand was big, solid, and warm around hers—steady and calming. "I'm not."

"Well, you must know I won't hurt you, so what should I think? You're afraid of the way you feel?"

He rubbed his thumbs softly over her knuckles. Some confession was due here, she admitted, and the contact helped. "Yes. There's that," she said quietly, looking at their linked hands. Hers looked so pale and petite in his. "I've got some very strong ideas about my life and how I want to live it, and the order in which I think things should be done." The words sounded so cold and calculated to her in this setting. "That's all being a bit threatened right now."

"By me? I'm not asking you to change your life."

In a way, he was right. He wasn't asking her to change her life. He didn't realize what he *was* asking of her. He couldn't. He was asking her to give him a piece of her heart. She wasn't sure what that entailed, and she'd feel ridiculous asking for an explanation of his intent.

In any case, starting any kind of personal relationship was too much right now. He didn't know what she'd been through. He couldn't see how he would affect her life, her career. He couldn't see that once the dam in her heart broke, once she gave in, her carefully laid plans could be washed away, her identity and future with them. Her mother had warned her, told her how she'd almost lost herself that way to her father. Her mother had almost ended up with nothing after her father left them. She'd warned Taryn, told her to build her career before giving her heart away.

And her mother's advice was the only scrap of family life Taryn could still cling to.

Worse, perhaps, was the fear that Douglas may end up rejecting her, and breaking her heart. She'd seen how her father had crushed her mother.

No, Douglas couldn't see any of that.

And he couldn't see that she was, regardless, falling in love with him.

How the hell did this happen? Her breath caught in her throat.

"Aren't you even a bit curious about where this could go?"

Curiosity killed the cat, she thought with nervous flippancy. "At this point in my life, I can't take that risk."

"What risk?" He let go of her hands and rose, walking over to the window, raking his hand through his hair again—

once, twice, three times. "Damn it, Taryn." He turned and walked back, movements jerked, aggravated, and thumped onto the chair again. "I sound like I'm begging for a date. This is ridiculous. What the devil are you so afraid of?"

She shook her head. "Douglas, I've got baggage. And I've got stuff to prove to myself too, before I can involve anyone else in my life."

He looked at her thoughtfully, searching her face. "We all have baggage," he finally said. His voice was calmer now; deep and smooth like a gentle caress. "Like what?"

"Things I need to deal with."

"There's someone else?"

"No. Some of the things relate to my old job—the job I want back—that don't seem to want to go away, won't be resolved for me until I go back." She wondered if she should tell Douglas about the situation with Todd, if only to explain why she'd gone into near hysterics twice already when she felt he'd pinned her in some way. But her pride wouldn't let her. Her conscience and her sense of professionalism told her it was something she'd need to deal with on her own.

"That goes hand in hand with the 'something to prove' I suppose." Restless, agitated, Douglas rose and walked to the window again. His jaw was clenched tight, she noticed.

"And there's some personal stuff, and how it would look to the staff if we . . . and there's my career to think of . . ." She let the words hang. *What the heck am I doing? I'm falling in love with this man, and I'm turning him down. When did I become such a coward?*

He turned to face her, shaking his head. "I think you're taking this far too seriously." He sat down again. "That's what's scaring you." He raised her chin with his finger, looking into her face. "Let's go for a ride and have a picnic somewhere." He leaned closer. "Come over to my place and let me make you dinner. Let me kiss you once in a while." With a soft feathery touch surprising in a man so strong, he traced her lips with his finger.

He pulled back then and gave her what he must have thought was an innocent smile. It wasn't innocent. Nothing about the man was innocent. "See," he said casually. "Nothing too serious."

She stared at him. Nothing too serious? The man made her head swim! She blinked a few times, trying to get her bearings. *There's too much at stake,* she reminded herself. He watched her, seeming to wait for a response. *But you can't throw this away. Think. Solve it. Think.*

Somehow, out of the murky swirl that now filled her tired brain, she came up with what, in that instant at least, seemed a good idea. "Maybe you're right," she said suddenly. "Maybe we could give it a try, you know, after my contract here ends. It's not so long now, and Vancouver isn't that far, when you think of it." The whole business with Hagen would have blown over by then, she assumed. If all went well, she'd have her new job and her career would be on track. They could see each other on weekends and such. She felt a sense of relief that she wouldn't be throwing this away. "We could . . . Douglas?"

He was eyeing her strangely, his mouth tightening with displeasure, his eyes no longer warm and inviting. He rose, rubbing his hand firmly on the back of his neck.

"Douglas?"

"Damn it Taryn." His breath came out in a rush, as if he'd been holding it. "I'm a patient man, but I'm not a saint. Maybe I'm mistaken." He frowned at her. "I must be, I guess, if you can suggest that we work together, platonically, for the next couple of months and then automatically switch to something more romantic once you're three hundred miles away. We're not talking about changing gears like a car. At least I'm not. Maybe it's just me. I was wrong once before."

She was confused at how her idea had backfired. It had seemed the perfect solution, in the heat of the moment. Proposing it had immediately eased her fears. But now that she thought about it, it did sound odd, and rather cold. "I thought—"

"I can see what you thought," he said sharply. "Thinking, thinking." He shook his head. "You're making me nuts with it. What about how you feel, how I feel? What about how you tremble when I kiss you? I've never met a woman so ready to deny her own feelings. I can help you get over whatever you're afraid of Taryn, but not if you won't let me." He swung his chair back to its spot beside the closet door.

Taryn could hear Hans and Gertrude in the hallway. Their noisy chatter shattered the intimacy already splintering around her. She suddenly felt like a toy boat bobbing adrift in the middle of a lake.

She heard him greet Hans and Gertrude as he quietly shut the door.

Chapter Eight

I *blew it.* Taryn rolled over in bed, wincing as her muscles protested the previous day's riding. The events funnelled into that one crashing thought, arriving like a physical blow. She stared blankly at the pale patterns the morning sunlight cast on the ceiling. *What a disaster.*

She bit her lip, rolled out of bed with a groan, and began pulling the new day's clothes into order. Busy; she had to get busy. A denim skirt landed on the bed.

But the thoughts fired relentlessly. Was she crazy? She couldn't leave it like that. Last night she'd finally admitted to herself that she was falling in love with him. How could she walk away from that? She'd proposed the idea about delaying their dating as a compromise, after he'd traced her lips in that most sensual way. How was a woman to think straight after such a thing?

She yanked a red cotton blouse from its hanger and flung it onto the bed too. For heaven's sake, he just wanted to see her, after all. He'd said himself that she was taking it too seriously. Couldn't she just have dinner with him, picnic with him, share a kiss or two? Why did she always need to make a big production out of everything? Cut it, dry it, analyze it, then pulverize it. Ridiculous. Maybe, just this once, she'd go with the flow. Gently and slowly. *Am I ready?*

She bent into the closet with a grunt, looking for her red leather sandals. On the other hand, if he really felt as he said he did, then why the hell couldn't he respect her feelings enough to delay the romantics until she finished her contract? Did he need to know the reasons she needed to wait? If they were legitimate for her, shouldn't that be good enough for him? Was there a time limit on his attraction to her? If so, then she'd end up with a broken heart anyway.

Arrrrgh! I'm driving myself insane! She tossed first one sandal then the other onto the floor behind her. She needed to talk with him first thing this morning and try to make things right. Somehow. He may feel differently this morning too. They were both exhausted last night. Exhausted and frustrated.

Taryn descended the stairs a short time later, a little slower than usual as her muscles continued to proclaim their discontent. Within minutes she was in her office, hands wrapping a steaming mug of tea, lamenting the fact that she'd come too late to get a fresh muffin. Today the tray had been empty. "The early bird . . ." she muttered to herself as Margaret walked in.

"Good mornin' to ye Taryn." Margaret slid the latest guest invoices onto Douglas's desk.

Taryn smiled. Margaret's cheery presence was a great way to start any day. "Good morning. And thanks for those, Margaret." She nodded toward the invoices. "By any chance, have you seen Douglas? I need to talk with him."

Margaret, already on her way out, paused in the doorway. "Oh, aye. As a matter of fact he was here this morning, about an hour ago. Took all the muffins, the rascal did."

"He what? Why?"

Margaret laughed. "He claimed them for the cowboys at summer camp. Said he was heading up there today. Anyone going up to camp always takes whatever baking Gertrude's done. Can't arrive without at least some cookies or the cowboys will send him back. It's become some kind of a tradition. Funny, though," she pursed her lips thoughtfully, "usually he lets Gertrude know in advance so she can make extra. But this time he didn't. I guess it must have been a spur of the moment decision for him to go." She laughed again. "Tina and Susan chased him to his truck, trying to get him to leave a few, but he was too fast."

"What's summer camp?" Taryn asked, less concerned with the food pilfering than with Douglas's sudden departure.

"That's where the cowboys live when the cattle are in the summer pasture, the high ground. It's about two hours' rough drive from here, on the back roads."

"Did he say when he'd be back?"

Margaret shrugged. "Nay. Probably a week or so. That's usual."

A week! "Why did he go? I mean, was there an emergency?"

"Not that I know of." She frowned. "I think we'd have heard if there were." She shrugged. "Sometimes the lads just go and help out." She winked then and added, "And sometimes I think they go for a break. You young people might call it 'male bonding.'" She spoke the expression carefully as if practicing a foreign language.

"I see." Taryn tried not to show her disappointment—Disappointment that was slowly developing into anger. "Thanks Margaret."

"He'll be back, dearie," Margaret said reassuringly from the doorway. "Don't ye worry." She checked behind her as if to ensure no one was there, then leaned into the room and whispered, "They tend to wander off by themselves when they get like that."

Taryn's eyes widened in surprise.

"He'll be back. And more himself then, I reckon."

"Uhh, yes, of course," Taryn all but stuttered, puzzled at Margaret's words, and her consoling tone. She stared after the floral apron as Margaret departed. Had Taryn sounded worried? Did the whole place know what was going on—or not going on—between herself and Douglas? Oh heck, she hoped not.

She shook it off and turned her attention to Douglas's desk. All caught up. Nothing outstanding. He must have worked half the night.

She sank into the chair and drummed her fingers on the smooth oak desktop. All that talk about getting something started with her, and boom—when he finds out she wouldn't be as easy as he'd hoped, he takes off. How, if he'd meant what he'd said, could he have left things like that last night? All those lofty claims about great potential and he couldn't even face her this morning to clear the air! And meanwhile, her own mind whirled for hours, depriving her of sleep, driving her half insane with questions and answers on how to remedy the situation. She had wanted to fix this. He obviously didn't.

"Bah!" She frowned into her cup and gulped another mouthful of tea. Well, he'd made things rather clear for her. The rat. To work, then, she told herself, as she began pulling files from her in-tray. Enough brain energy wasted on this. He was gone. She grabbed the phone and dialed her first business call of the day—quickly, before the lump in her throat got too big to swallow.

Thirty minutes and three calls later, her mind comfortably, if temporarily, distracted by her work, she paused as a flash of pink caught her eye. A tiny vase holding a single pink rose stood at the corner of her desk, almost blocked by some binders Margaret had brought in. A sigh of pleasure escaped her. The bright pink petals proclaimed a fresh summer beauty, so striking against the sterility of the office. Gordon's roses, she thought fondly, remembering the profusion of

pink she had seen in the inn's gardens. Gordon arranged
small bouquets of flowers for each table in the dining room
every day. Taryn smiled, thinking that today of all days she
appreciated his gesture. The flower symbolized a fresh perspective. And she certainly needed that this morning. She'd
have to remember to thank him the next time she saw him.

A late supper consisting of a sandwich and some carrot
sticks sat unfinished on the corner of her desk. Finally satisfied that all details for the Randolf wedding were captured
on the lists in her files, Taryn cleaned up her papers and prepared to call it a day. She looked at her watch. Ten o'clock
already. She rose carefully from her chair, rubbing the stiff-
ness from the small of her back. At least her leg muscles had
finally stopped aching—getting relief from that had taken
several days! She made a mental note to tell Douglas, some-
time, that his ointment had done her little good.

The inn had quieted down, weeknights being early ones
even for the few overnight guests. Taryn hugged herself and
leaned against the filing cabinet, eyes closed, tilting her head
back to absorb the sounds. Something about these evenings
in the small office comforted her, relaxed her, regardless of
the paperwork stacked on her desk. She loved the snaps,
creaks, and groans of the old inn settling in for the night, the
occasional muffled footsteps from upstairs, and the gentle
murmur of voices from the saloon, sometimes punctuated by
bursts of hearty laughter as guests shared jokes and stories.

Sounds from the dining room and kitchen, faint but dis-
tinctive from her office, created a comfortable homey feeling. She noticed the clinking of china and silver, the squeak-
ing of the swinging doors as staff passed between kitchen
and dining room. She inhaled deeply. Delicious aromas
always wafted through the building, lingering from late din-
ners. Tonight she detected barbecued ribs, grilled steak, and
now freshly baked apple pie.

She realized the old inn already felt more like home than any of the other places she had lived. She allowed herself a rueful smile. Her situation here was storybook perfect from a child's perspective, wasn't it? She had her own beautiful room, lots of interesting things to keep her busy, a big yard and garden to enjoy, horses, the lake. Her best friend lived a few steps away. Margaret and Gordon MacKay made the perfect parental figures—loving, busy, fussy about the building and the grounds. They reminded her of Mr. and Mrs. Claus; plump, rosy-cheeked, caring, and giving. And, when she let her guard down, she was falling in love with the proverbial boy next door—well, sort of next door.

No point in fantasizing. She stopped herself short. She wasn't a child, and this was her temporary job, not her permanent home. She had a career to build, after all. And the boy next door was a hot-blooded, handsome man, possessing a potent magnetism that had already caused her to doubt herself and her priorities, driving her half-crazy. And worse, when he didn't get what he wanted from her, he'd left. Five days now, and the hurt still felt raw.

She grimaced, squeezing her eyes shut, resting her head back against the top drawer. She pressed her fingers to her temples and wished she could turn her mind off.

"I liked the part where you smiled much better," a smooth, low voice said quietly from beside her.

Taryn's eyes flew open as she started, slamming her hands back against the cabinet to keep her balance. "You gave me a bloody heart attack! Don't go sneaking up on people like that!"

Douglas smiled and spun his office chair around to straddle it. "I didn't sneak. You were a million miles away. What are you still doing here?"

"Just on my way up to bed, actually." She moved away from the filing cabinet. Uncertainty drained the grace from her movements.

Douglas's hand came out and caught hers. She swallowed

hard, trying to read his mood. Should she broach the subject of their disastrous discussion now? Or, for tonight, should she leave well enough alone? There were dark shadows under his eyes and lines of fatigue etched on either side of his mouth. The hint of a dark beard stubbled his face, giving him a rough, roguish air, like an outlaw in a western movie. She watched his eyes search her face, but his expression gave nothing away.

"Come with me. Outside." He rose and tugged gently at her arm. "I want to show you something." He stepped past her, pulling her along behind him through the office door.

"Not submarine races, I hope," she mumbled, resisting slightly. *Oh nuts, now I'm babbling. Pull it together.*

He laughed. "No. The Northern Lights. *Aurora borealis.* We don't see them often this far south. Come on," he coaxed. "The fresh air will do you good."

Propelled more by curiosity than by Douglas's towing, she let him lead her toward the inn's back porch. The first thing she noticed when they stepped out into the cool night air was the glow of Gordon's pink roses in the moonlight, almost eerie with brightness against the black night. She paused, staring.

"They're catching some of the aurora's light," Douglas remarked, following her gaze. "Spooky, isn't it?" He let go of her hand and moved to the side railing, leaning out. "Come," he motioned. "You can see from here."

She saw the radiant splendor in the sky behind him as she approached. Her breath caught sharply as she leaned out from under the porch roof, the north sky opening to her view. Huge panels of sheer pastels—green, pink, blue—pulsed and danced like curtains in a breeze. Their boundaries evaporated and reappeared, their cores undulated as though heaven itself were breathing life into them. She'd never seen such a thing, and she stared, open-mouthed, as the alien beauty of it filled her senses. Caught up in the spectacle, she almost jumped when Douglas spoke.

"What do you think?" His voice was quiet, befitting a comment made in the presence of the seemingly holy event before them.

"Awesome," she whispered. She felt his body behind hers now. Close, but not touching. They stood that way for some time, Taryn mesmerized by the majesty of heaven's living art. "It's like magic," she finally said.

Douglas leaned over slightly, placing his hands on the railing on either side of her waist. She spun around in surprise, and found herself enveloped in his arms. Her gaze flew to his face and found his eyes on hers; a small smile played at his mouth. He raised his eyebrows as if in challenge.

She felt the railing, rigid against her back. The solid wall of his body loomed just inches in front of her and, without touching her, his strong arms held her in on either side. Butterflies took flight in her stomach.

He studied her face. "Now what, Taryn?"

He smelled wonderful, like the forest, with a hint of his usual sandalwood and the slightest tang of male sweat. "Douglas . . ." The word held wariness, a warning.

"Douglas what?" he whispered. "Douglas I was wrong? Douglas I've missed you? Douglas kiss me?" His lips moved to touch her earlobe—not a kiss, not a nibble, just a touch—and dissolved her thoughts. She swayed to the right, away from the sensation and leaned into the steely support of his left forearm. "Douglas what?" he repeated.

She bit her lip and turned back to the dancing lights. *Where is all the air? Why can't I breathe?* Douglas didn't move. Taryn crossed her arms, looking out at the colors surging above. "Your sudden departure after our talk . . . It hurt," she finally said.

He was quiet for a moment. "So did your refusal. I thought it best to give you some time. Some space. And me too." His words barely moved her hair; his breath warmed her scalp.

"I didn't want time or space. I wanted to make it right." She shivered as she spoke, but not from the cold. His hands moved to her arms, as if to warm her. She watched the lights billow in the sky, unsure of what to say next. *I can't very well tell someone that I'm falling in love with him and in the same breath tell him I'm not ready for a relationship!*

"You can have your compromise, Taryn," Douglas finally said.

She half turned in surprise. "Really?"

"Sure. But I'm asking you for a compromise too."

"And what's that?" she asked cautiously.

"You might want to delay any romantics until your contract ends, but that doesn't mean I have to." He must have felt her flinch, because he quickly added, "Not completely, that is. I'll wait that long for you to respond in kind, if I have to, but in the meantime, I'll just continue to court you. Unless you come right out and tell me to go to hell." He quirked a brow in challenge.

She opened her mouth to speak, then snapped it shut again, puzzled.

"I'll be discreet, so your professional image will remain unscathed," he added with exaggerated formality, "so don't worry about that." He rubbed his hands up and down her arms, then let them drop to wrap loosely around her waist. As she stiffened in shock, he smoothly turned her body toward him, and gave her a quick kiss.

She was too surprised to respond, and when he pulled back she had to grip the railing behind her to regain her balance. She stared at him, head cocked, still speechless, trying to make sense of this turn of events.

"Just a trial run," he said casually, though his breathing had quickened and she could see the pulse beating fast in his throat. "Someone might see, after all."

"Some compromise," she said with forced sarcasm, trying to steady herself.

He chuckled softly. "I thought so."

"What if I don't agree?"

"I didn't think you would." He appeared to dismiss her comment, changing the subject. "Maybe you should head up to bed. I guess we've got some work to go over in the morning before I head back to camp."

"Douglas, that's not going to work very well," she protested as he took her arm, leading her back inside.

He seemed—rather pretended, she suspected—not to hear her. "Charlie broke his arm while I was up there," he continued conversationally, as if nothing unusual had happened between them. "We've got a new guy coming in a few days, but they're a man short if I don't go back."

She stepped through the door, wondering how he could be so calm and casual. "You don't need to see me to my door, Douglas. I can manage from here." She stood on the stair and faced him at eye level so he couldn't miss her words. "I have to say, I'm not comfortable with your version of this compromise." She wouldn't be able to function if he were trying to romance her at every turn, but she couldn't very well tell him to 'go to hell,' as he'd so bluntly put it. Was it this or nothing?

He lifted his shoulder, and she detected a distinct glint in his eye. "All's fair in love and war."

"And just which of those would you call this?"

He grinned. "That, Sweetheart, is up to you."

Chapter Nine

Taryn paused on the last rise before the trail dipped toward the inn, taking a moment to catch her breath. The sunset cast a golden glow over the sun-bleached hillsides, deepening the vivid greens of the golf course and the rich reds of the barns. The lake, much of it already in shadow, seemed to have pulled the remaining light into itself, as if storing the source for the night to come. A beautiful place, she thought again, glad to have taken time for an evening walk.

Later, as she came through the inn's gardens, she saw Alison waving to her impatiently from the inn's steps. "C'mon Taryn, there's an important phone call for you!"

Taryn took the steps two at a time and grabbed the receiver on the reception desk. Alison was right at her heels, chewing furiously on her lower lip.

"Taryn Christiansen speaking."

A few minutes later, having jotted down a message, Taryn replaced the receiver, pulling her brows together.

"Well?" Alison prompted anxiously.

"It was Walter Dennison from Thompson Trust."

"Yes. I know. That's why I knew it was important. What did he want?"

"There appears to be a problem with the inn's loan,"

119

Taryn relayed, watching as Alison's frown deepened. "He wanted to talk with Douglas or Fred, but of course they aren't here, so he hoped I could help him. I can't. Have you heard from Douglas?"

Alison shook her head. Taryn reached over and rubbed Alison's brow with her thumb. "They'll work it out. Stop frowning, you'll get wrinkles." She hoped that encouraging Alison would ease her own worries. "C'mon into the coffee shop with me for some iced tea."

"Ahh, hello Taryn." Margaret's sturdy, round frame swept into the coffee shop with a tray of dishes; her bright floral apron reflected her usual sunny expression. "Hello to ye too, Alison." She leaned over the counter and set her load down with a clatter. "Come see me when ye're done with Ali, Taryn, and I'll catch you up on the Randolf wedding arrangements—no, all's well," she added wagging a finger to stop Taryn's instant concern. "I just got the guest list for those who'll be stayin' here at the inn. I'll be at the front desk."

Taryn turned to Alison with a smile. "I guess I'd better be off. I can't believe the wedding's only three days away now—actually the arrival of guests is only two days away." She ran her fingers through her hair, massaging the back of her neck a bit to ease the tension suddenly growing there. "If we get through this, we can get through anything."

"I think that's the idea, financially anyway," Alison said cheerfully, pulling her weight slowly out of the chair. "Gosh, this babe's getting heavy." She rubbed her tummy lovingly. "Not long to go now." She turned quickly and looked at Taryn. "You'll be here for the birth, won't you?"

Taryn did a quick mental calculation as they walked onto the shadowed porch. "I'll be back in Vancouver already." At Alison's stricken expression she added reassuringly, "Just call me the moment you go into labor and I'll be here in four hours."

"Your contract?"

"You're due at the beginning of October. My contract is until the end of September, at the end of the season. I'll have to go back to Vancouver to work, if not at the Stanley Park Hotel, then . . ." she shrugged, leaving the sentence unfinished. "Anyway," she squeezed Alison's hand, "I'll come as soon as you call."

Alison descended the few steps and turned. "I can't see how you'd want to leave this place. You're doing great. What about the winter retreat idea? I can't see how Fred wouldn't give you the benefit of the doubt if you said you could make this place turn a profit in the winter."

Taryn laughed. "We'll see." Alison's confidence in her abilities was heart-warming. Her elbow brushed the climbing roses on the railing and she suddenly noticed their light fragrance on the evening air. "Why are you looking at me like that?" She questioned Alison's wide-eyed stare and surprised smile and suddenly sensed a presence behind her. Without even turning around, she knew Douglas stood behind her.

"Hi Douglas," Alison waved. "Got to go, Taryn."

"I've been looking for you." Douglas's voice, low and smooth, seemed to reverberate through her body, like leaning against a large stereo speaker during a song with heavy bass.

"Hello Douglas," she said. *Be cool, calm, and collected.* She stuffed her hands into her pockets. That, at least, would stop her from fidgeting. She looked up into his eyes and felt her heart lurch.

His gaze scanned her face. "A little flushed," he said softly, "but otherwise as beautiful as ever. Ready to come over for dinner yet?" he teased.

Warning bells sounded in her head as she gauged his flirtatious mood. His warped version of her compromise had, surprisingly, worked fairly well so far. Admittedly, they hadn't spent much time alone together. During what Taryn had come to term as their 'public' time, the undercurrent of attraction seemed stronger now, likely because of the taboo of its expression. The man could flirt with his eyes. He could stand just a little too close for too long. He could play by the rules and still turn her defences to sand. And the few times he'd cornered her alone just about undid the merits of his 'good' public behavior. His most recent kiss, unanticipated and fleeting as she'd left the stables after delivering a message to Barrel, still felt warm on her lips. And that was yesterday! She'd come upon him by accident, as she passed Sergeant's stall calling Barrel. Without saying a word, he reached for her hand, pulled her close, and kissed her before she knew what was happening. He had released her quickly and resumed his work with Sergeant only a second before Barrel came around the corner to answer her call.

"I should update you on the Randolf wedding," she said abruptly.

"Ah, right, the big day's almost here," he said resignedly, obviously recognizing her refusal to be drawn into banter. "What are you drinking?" he asked, eyeing her empty glass. "I'll get us more." When he returned, he was all business.

"There ye are!" The screen door creaked open and Margaret stuck her head out. "Oh, hello Douglas. Good to see ye again laddie. Ye're finally back, I'm glad."

"Thanks, Margaret," he said. His business mood evaporated. "Ye didn't seem to suffer any in my absence." He took Margaret's hand. "Looking as lovely as ever, ye are. That Gordon must be takin' good care of ye." Douglas's imitation of Margaret's Scottish brogue was excellent. Taryn was also astounded at his playfulness. She had never seen this side of him before, or the quick switch between business and fun.

Margaret tittered, blushing furiously. "Oh, Douglas, just ye behave," she reprimanded without sincerity. She turned to Taryn, still smiling, and held out a file folder.

"Oh my gosh. I'm sorry Margaret. I was supposed to

come and see you about the guest list and it slipped my mind." Taryn took the file with thanks, flipping it open.

"Not to worry, dear. If I were twenty-five years younger and had this handsome devil show up on me porch, I'd be forgettin' too."

Taryn looked up in surprise and saw Douglas grin and wink at Margaret. She stared at him for a moment. Handsome devil indeed, she thought. He was relaxed and confident in the big wicker chair, one foot resting on his knee, spotted with trail dust, jeans and T-shirt strained in all the right places. Her gaze moved back to his face and she cringed inwardly. He was staring right back at her, those gray eyes seeing into her very soul. She felt her stomach drop and quickly looked at Margaret, who sent a knowing smile back at her. She felt a blush begin and tried to concentrate on the business at hand.

Thinking better of trying to deny what was so obviously true, she returned her attention to the contents of the file. "Anyone in here we should know about?"

Margaret perched herself on the third wicker chair and cleared her throat slightly, catching both Douglas and Taryn's attention. "Well, Douglas . . ." she began.

"Let me see." Douglas leaned onto Taryn's arm as he looked at the list. A moment later he groaned, his expression tightening.

"What is it?" Taryn asked.

Douglas and Margaret looked at each other. "It's amazing where some people turn up, isn't it?" Douglas's expression darkened further.

"Who?" Taryn's curiosity sharpened.

"Carla Fairbanks." Douglas said the name with some distaste. He suddenly looked very tired, resting his head on the back of the chair.

Carla. Why did that name sound familiar? Of course, Douglas's ex-fiancée! The thought of this woman returning to the inn, to Douglas's proximity, raised Taryn's ire. The effect her coming was having on Douglas's mood also stirred a surprisingly possessive reaction within her. Could it be that there were still sparks between them? Carla had left him, after all. *Sparks? Look at the man. He's a walking butane lighter. Just look at how quickly I lit up, surrounded by my bastion of professionalism.*

He tilted his head and looked thoughtfully at the ceiling. "Something's up."

"Now, Douglas, ye don't know that she hasn't changed. She may have met someone else and started a whole new life." Margaret interceded.

Douglas held up his hand in defence. "Margaret, you're a love for giving her the benefit of the doubt, but if she'd met someone else and made a new start, she wouldn't be coming back here for a social event."

Margaret sighed in resignation. "Well," she tried again, "she is sharing a room with this Todd Hagen fellow. He must be her new beau—"

Taryn choked on her iced tea, but managed to recover after only a few coughs and sputters. "I'm fine," she croaked, waving off both Douglas's and Margaret's looks of concern. She hadn't given any thought to the fact that, as a close friend of the Randolf family, Todd would be at the wedding. And of course Todd would be staying on site rather than in town. But sleeping with Douglas's ex-fiancée . . . Could the world be any smaller?

She felt Douglas's hand suddenly cover her own, gripping her glass. The contact made her jump.

"Taryn, the idea is to hold the glass upright so the liquid stays inside," he said with a small smile, turning her wrist to stop the silent flow of tea onto the porch.

"Oh!" She set the glass down quickly. "How stupid of me."

"You know this Todd fellow?" Douglas asked as she mopped the spill with napkins.

She straightened and cleared her throat, feeling that

cursed blush rising to her face again. "Yes. I worked with him at the Stanley Park Hotel," she answered simply.

Douglas watched her intently. Taryn offered nothing else, turning her attention to Margaret, who rose to leave.

"I've still got a few things to do," Margaret said. "Let me know if you need anything else, or," she pointed to the list, "if you want to change any of the room arrangements I've made." The screen door bounced shut behind her.

Douglas was still staring at her. "And?"

"His name is Todd Hagen, as you can see on the sheet."

"Is that name supposed to mean something to me?"

"Hagen, as in the Hagen family that owns the Stanley Park Hotel and a number of other hotels in North America. They have many other business ventures as well. Todd is the nephew of the owner of the company, being groomed for some top executive spot." She tried to keep the sarcasm out of her voice.

"You don't like him."

"No." She set her glass down and leaned back in her chair, willing herself to relax. "He was a key factor in my not getting my promotion, in my having to leave the hotel."

"I get the feeling it's more than that. Romantic attachment?"

She suddenly felt like he was grilling her, and it got her back up. "Not on my part."

He raised his brows at that. "Interesting answer."

She shrugged her shoulders, agitated, wanting to divert his questioning. "And now he's rather close with your ex-fiancée. So, what kind of trouble are you anticipating?"

Douglas ran a hand through his hair and exhaled. "I have no idea. It just doesn't sit well with me. Even less now that I know she's involved with such a powerful family. She's a lawyer." It was the only other information he offered.

Taryn suddenly remembered the telephone call from the trust company. "Oh, I almost forgot," she said, rising. "I left a note on your desk. Mr. Dennison called from Thompson Trust. He wanted to talk with you—said it was important."

"Yeah, I gather it is pretty important," Douglas said, unfolding his frame from the chair. "I'd better call him right away."

Moments later Taryn entered the office just as Douglas hung up the telephone. "Bloody hell," he muttered, throwing his pen onto the desk and glaring at it.

She dropped a stack of files onto her desk and began flipping through them, looking for the wedding flower orders to give them a final check. "What's up?" She continued her search, waiting for his reply.

He sat completely still, staring at the pen, for at least a full minute before she looked up again.

"Douglas, what is it? About the loan?" She saw his shoulders rise and fall on a deep breath. She stopped her search and waited, watching him, now more than a little worried.

He was quiet for a few moments more before turning to her, his expression dark, the lines around his mouth and eyes etched deeper than before. "It's been a hell of a few weeks," was all he said, looking away again.

"You look exhausted." *What's going on?*

"You and I need to talk, Taryn."

Even in her limited experience with men, she knew they rarely spoke the words "we need to talk." This had to be important. Maybe his mood had nothing to do with the call. Perhaps he was tired of their arrangement? Perhaps, faced with the return of his ex-fiancée, he'd just come to terms with some old feelings for Carla? They had a big weekend ahead, one that seemed to have become a microcosm for the inn's future prospects. They needed to free themselves of as much emotional baggage as possible in order to direct all energies to the wedding. "Yes, I guess we do."

Douglas's eyebrows raised slightly. "So you know what this is about," he stated, not really forming a question.

Did the man think she was dense? "I have a pretty good idea." She slid into her chair and propped her chin on her hands.

"No, not here," he said grimly. "I don't want anyone over-hearing this." He pushed his chair back and got to his feet. "Let's go."

"Where are we going?" she asked, rising slowly. She wasn't sure if going somewhere with him was such a good idea. The business environment was definitely the safest. "I'd prefer to discuss it here."

"No." He held the office door open and gestured impatiently with his head. "We'll take a walk along the lake."

"But it's getting dark out." Taryn moved to the door but held back, surprised, when his hand propped her elbow and urged her through. "Do you mind?" She pulled her arm free. "I can walk well enough on my own."

He looked straight ahead as they walked—no, marched—along the lakeside path. The change from evening to night was almost complete, and Taryn had to watch her step carefully in the semi-darkness. A cool wind had kicked up, tossing Taryn's curls into her eyes. She brushed them away impatiently.

She felt tense now, away from the security of the inn. It didn't help that her nervous attempts at small talk were met with one or two-word replies from Douglas. She'd never seen him like this. After three tries, she gave up. They continued along the water's edge, the silence broken only by their feet crunching on the gravel path and the waves lapping the shoreline.

"Well?" Taryn could no longer stand it. She slowed her step. He glanced at her and kept walking.

"At least slow down. This isn't a race." She was growing increasingly anxious. "Douglas, you're scaring me. Stop. What is it?"

He slowed his step and turned, looking over her head toward the inn. "It's beautiful, isn't it?"

Her gaze followed his for a moment. She realized that she'd never seen the inn at night, with the lights from its many windows glowing in warm welcome. "Absolutely gorgeous," she agreed, turning to search his face for a clue to his dark mood.

"I spoke with Mr. Dennison." He continued to look past her. "From Thompson Trust," he added needlessly.

"Yes," she said. *And?*

"It seems there's a problem with our loan payments—for the inn." He looked down at her, eyes intent.

She gave him a blank look, pushing her bangs out of her eyes again.

"We borrowed money to keep the inn afloat while we worked on improving the way it was run," he expanded. "It was a few years ago and we've tried a few things that didn't work all that well. Now we have you." He gave her a small smile that didn't reach his eyes. She raised her brows expectantly.

"Thompson Trust has had its own financial difficulties lately," he continued, starting to walk again, but more slowly this time. "They've been good to us, letting us schedule our loan repayments on a very flexible plan, even when they were suffering. We renew the re-payment terms every year, gauging how everyone's faring. It's always been a really friendly exchange. They're from Kamlen, a fairly small town, and people around here stick together." He glanced at her, and she looked back at him, still uncomfortable with his grim expression.

"Thompson Trust has just been bought out by a larger company." His voice carried a hard edge now. He stopped and turned to her, eyes dark and cold. Taryn felt a chill of foreboding run down her spine as he trapped her gaze with his. "This larger company is making some drastic changes in the way they want to see loans repaid, including ours. No grace periods. No flexibility. The take-over will be complete in about a month, just about the time we would have decided upon our repayment terms for the coming year. Their new loan repayment plan starts then." He waited a moment, watching as she digested the information.

"What about using ranch money to—"

He cut her off. "The ranch is just hanging on these past few years, with the price of beef in one of its cyclical lows. It just can't keep carrying the inn as a liability. It's too expensive and makes bad business sense, especially since we don't know how long it will take beef prices to recover. The ranch has sixty thousand acres and over twenty-six hundred cows—key assets that we just can't jeopardize to keep the inn going. So, if they foreclose, that's it for the inn being ours. They'll take it over; maybe sell it, maybe run it themselves." Douglas paused.

He seemed to be waiting for her to comment. Taryn didn't know what to say. She pulled her gaze away and looked at the inn for a long moment, absorbing just how much the place and the people associated with it had come to mean to her. If there was a threat to it, she knew she would fight tooth and nail like the rest of the community to save it.

She looked back at him, staring at the hard line of his mouth to avoid the chill emanating from his eyes, wishing she could remove the pain she saw there. She tried to form what she hoped was a reassuring smile. "It doesn't sound good Douglas, but business is picking up. We're not that short on our loan payments, are we? And what do you mean they might run it themselves?"

"No, we're not that short on our loan payments, and business is picking up. Your ads and ideas are showing an improvement in business already," he said. But it didn't sound like much of a compliment, more like a trivial fact. "What they might do is foreclose on us before we even get

our feet on the ground, before we can even make the inn
meet the new repayment schedule."

"Why would they do that?" Taryn frowned. "Financial
companies don't want to run country inns. They want their
clients to do well in their businesses. Foreclosure usually
isn't a very profitable venture."

"I'm not surprised that you know so much about it," he
said with a sardonic smile.

She paused, wondering what that comment meant. Why
was she getting such anger from him? She'd never seen him
so upset. "I don't understand what's gotten into you."

"A financial company didn't buy Thompson Trust, Taryn."
This is getting bizarre. "What? Who then?"

"You claim not to know?"

"Would you just tell me what the heck you're getting at?"

"Hagen Enterprises bought Thompson Trust."

She gave him a blank look as the information sank in and
settled like a stone in her chest.

"Hagen Enterprises, as in the same company that owns
the Stanley Park Hotel and a number of other hotels, not to
mention an assortment of other businesses, as you explained
a little while ago."

Taryn put her hands on her hips, staring at him in shock.
"Hagen Enterprises bought Thompson Trust and is now trying to foreclose on the inn? Why?" she asked, sickened by
the feeling that she already knew.

"That's the word from Dennison," he said coldly, and
began walking again. "You tell me. You're the one who
worked for them. You're the one who came here to bring the
place into the black. I'm thinking some pretty awful stuff
here Taryn. I've been given the impression that you might be
testing it for them. And thanks to you, they now see that it's
possible, that it could be profitable." He looked away. "We
won't willingly sell, especially if it's doing better—they
know that—but there's a small window of opportunity for
them to foreclose on us if we don't meet the new loan repay-

ment schedule they're setting for us." He gave a small, humorless laugh.

"I'm thinking," Douglas continued coldly, slowing his stride, "that this might be the real reason you didn't want us—you and me—to get involved, why you wouldn't allow us to get something going, even though the attraction was as clear as the creek water. I'll bet you didn't bargain for that part when you took the job, did you? That you'd want me as much as I want you?"

His words stabbed Taryn right in the heart. Her own words lodged in her throat, jumbling into a thick, hard knot. She tried to swallow and nearly choked, stopping on the path with a hand on her neck. "You—you think I—?" she sputtered. *Todd! That bloody rat! I refused to give him the information he wanted, but he seemed to have found it on his own! And now Douglas thinks I . . .*

He spun and glared at her. "What am I supposed to think?" He raised open hands in exasperation. "Taryn, your name is on at least one of the feasibility reports. Dennison saw that himself. And he tells me Todd Hagen, the man dealing with him on this, mentioned your name like it was inside information. Ironic how his name just came up, there on the porch, isn't it?"

Damn him! Damn Todd! And damn Douglas for believing the worst. She was so hurt and angry she started to see black spots before her eyes. "You think *I* have something to do with Hagen buying Thompson Trust? You think *I'm* some kind of corporate spy? That they planted me here?" Her pitch increased to a near screech. She took a breath and held it, trying to calm herself.

"The circumstances are not in your favor here," Douglas all but shouted at her.

"Todd and I were co-workers. He did some rotten stuff to me, and I turned around and did something that made him very angry. I didn't think it would come to this—"

"What the hell is this?" He cut her off, so angry she wondered if he'd even heard her. He gestured between the two of them. "Between me and you? What did you think you could get by towing me along that you couldn't just get in the files? You had free access to everything."

Her jaw dropped in horror. He caught her wrist just before her hand connected with his cheek, clasping it in an iron grip. "Nice try. I don't let my guard down twice, in any area of my life," he added pointedly, then dropped her hand.

He turned away and paced a few steps before facing her again. "Listen, Taryn. I don't know what sick game this is, or how exactly you're involved. But you'll finish your contract. You'll get this place into a financial position leaving no chance for foreclosure. And I'll be watching you," he warned. "I'll not have my livelihood—the livelihood of my family and this whole community—threatened by the whims of some heartless big-city corporation. I've been burned before." He shook his head. "I can't give you the benefit of the doubt here. There's too much at stake."

His echo of her own words, part of the explanation she'd used as an excuse not to get involved with him, drove the knife in even deeper. She rubbed her wrist where he'd grasped it; the anger behind his grip hurt more than the grip itself had. "How could you believe—"

"I thought we had something, something to build on. But you held back—and that was just an excuse not to expect more from you. I can't believe I fell for it," Douglas said with disgust.

She stepped back quickly, regaining her balance, forcing her legs to support her. Nausea loomed; she wrapped an arm around her stomach, pressed her fingers to her lips, and looked at him, wondering if he could hear the sound of her heart tearing apart. A thousand thoughts raced through her mind, but her mouth could only form three little words: "Go to hell." She tried to pull herself together, straightening her back and forcing her head up. Then, with as much dignity as she could muster, she turned and walked away into the darkness, the lights from the inn acting as her homing beacon.

The tears came the moment she closed her bedroom door. She let them come, pressing her face into the fluffy pillows on her bed so that no one would hear. Exhaustion, stress, hurt, betrayal, the false accusations, and a love realized then sliced to shreds—everything piled into her heart at once; the weight was simply too much to bear.

She cried about things she had never cried about before— for her lonely childhood, her parents' divorce; for the sense of home she never really had; for the emptiness of her family life. Now, years later, the first tears flowed for the way neither of her parents seemed to have had time for her, even after their break-up, and for the constant moves and the lack of long-term friends which resulted. She cried for the great job she lost through no fault of her own at the Stanley Park Hotel; for the cruelty the Hagen fiasco had twisted into her life. She cried for Douglas and the love that may have been; for his willingness to believe the worst of her. And then the tears came for the realization that she was about to lose her beloved Aspen Creek, the place and the people that had become her heart's home.

Eventually the tears ran out, replaced by deep breaths, the occasional hiccup, and the beginning of a pounding headache. Taryn lay spent on the bed. She couldn't remember ever crying like that before, couldn't actually remember crying at all, except when she had fallen off her bicycle at the age of eight and ripped open her knee. But that had been a different pain—Strictly physical. She rolled over and stared at the ceiling, then lay her forearm across her eyes.

It was over, she told herself. Enough crying. She lay quietly for a while longer, letting the catharsis run its course. The only way out was through. It was time to re-focus on the work that needed to be done.

Chapter Ten

"Everything looks absolutely lovely," Mrs. Randolf gushed, fanning herself with what Taryn believed was a beautifully embroidered, Japanese-style, silk fan. It moved too quickly to identify, somewhat mesmerizing to her sleep-deprived senses, and made it difficult for her to concentrate, her brain being in a state of befuddlement ever since the encounter with Douglas two days before. She forced herself to focus on the woman's words.

"Thank you, Mrs. Randolf. Everything has been arranged to your specifications, and we added some of our own touches." She glanced at the fresh flowers adorning almost every surface in the reception area and the trails of daisies, roses, and ribbons gracing the staircase. Mrs. Randolf cooed her approval, the layers of her generous double chin folding and unfolding with the effort.

"Exquisite," she said with a smile. "And outside," she rolled her eyes heavenward, "just marvelous, Ms. Christiansen, just marvelous." She peered out the window to the garden area where Gordon and Margaret were setting up the pastor's podium and making final touches to the arrangement of white wooden chairs.

Explosions of fresh flowers stood in a row on small

pedestals, forming the aisle down which the bride and groom would walk. The podium was backed by the huge trellis supporting masses of Gordon's pink climbing roses. It was picture perfect, indeed. The sun shone brightly, with no threat of rain. And, for a change, it wasn't suffocatingly hot either. Warm, but not stifling. Taryn sighed. So far, so good. As Mrs. Randolf moved toward some friends, Taryn headed to the saloon to see if Susan and Tina needed any help at the bar.

"I'm telling you, I have nothing to do with it," a strong, obviously agitated female voice said. Taryn stopped. The voice had come from one of the small meeting rooms just ahead. The polished oak door stood slightly ajar.

"Somehow I find that surprising, Carla." Douglas's voice carried the same hard edge it had when he hurled his vicious accusations at Taryn two days ago. The tone set Taryn's nerves on edge.

"Look, why would you think I'd want anything to do with this place? I've spent enough time here. I've moved on, Douglas. The past is the past. Leave it there."

"Actually, I was hoping you would leave the past where it was, but then I find out that you're one of Hagen's lawyers. That connection is just a bit too coincidental. I want an explanation."

Taryn felt guilty, standing there in the hallway listening to the conversation, but could not bring her feet to move. Besides, she thought, they might see her if she walked by. She brushed the guilt aside and waited. After all, this had a lot to do with her.

"There's nothing to explain. Hagen Enterprises has more than one lawyer, you know. And I'm new there."

"You may not be working on it, but you can find out about it," Douglas countered. "It's Todd Hagen's project. Seems that you two are pretty tight these days."

"I don't know any more than you. He's into a lot of things and we haven't been seeing each other for very long, not that it's any of your business. And if I didn't know better, I'd say I just caught a note of jealousy," Carla challenged.

"You do know better," Douglas replied harshly. "I don't much care who you're seeing these days, but this guy is bad news for everyone here."

"What about your new manager?" Carla shot back. "Todd seems to know her pretty well. I hear they worked together, were pretty tight for awhile. Why aren't you pouncing down her neck?"

Silence. Pretty tight? What were people saying about her and Todd? Taryn wished she could see what was going on, see Douglas's expression. The fire was gone from his tone when he spoke again. "I *have* talked to her about it." He paused. "It's your angle I want right now."

His face must have said more than his words. "Oh my," Carla oozed, and Taryn imagined a smug smile on the woman's face, "the mighty have fallen. What's this? Courting the inn's manager, Dougie? Is there a pattern developing here?"

Taryn clutched the clipboard to her chest, straining to hear.

"Leave it," Douglas growled. "I want your angle."

A pause, then, "Fine, Fine. You don't have to make any confessions to me. But I told you, I don't know any more than you do about this take-over thing. Why don't you just believe me?"

"I gave up giving you the benefit of the doubt the day you left—the first time you left," he amended.

"I can't help—"

"You can find out," he interrupted.

"Leave me out of it."

"Hell, Carla, this was your home. Doesn't that mean anything?" He sounded exasperated now.

"And this is my new life. What if someone found out I was snooping and passing along privileged information? I'd lose my job and maybe my membership in the bar."

"Someone like Todd?" he asked sarcastically.

Carla lowered her voice. Taryn inched closer to the door.

"Todd is hungry," Carla was saying. "He's a climber. I'm going to stick with him for awhile. I think it's in my best interest."

They deserve each other! Taryn thought immediately.

"You two deserve each other," Douglas said with disgust, and Taryn smiled in spite of it all.

The two were quiet for a long moment. Taryn tensed. What was going on?

"Well?" Douglas's voice had softened.

"Look, if I find out something and it doesn't threaten my position, I'll pass it along to you." Carla's tone had lost its bluster as well. "For ol' times sake, to use one of your hokey expressions. Fair enough?"

"Humph," was Douglas's only response.

"It's not like I owe you any favors, Douglas. You were supposed to do me one, remember? You owed me. You gave me your word that you'd try the city. How long did that last? A month? Maybe two, before you were back here? You had a great job in a powerful accounting firm. I just can't understand why you tossed it for this."

"I kept my word, and don't ever think otherwise." His voice was low and strained. "Glenda was ill, for God's sake. Fred needed me, and I needed my family. My commuting didn't work. You came back too, remember? You agreed. And the next thing I knew you were gone. I don't think our location had anything to do with the fact that we were a mistake."

The door whipped open before Taryn could move, and she dropped her clipboard in shock. She stooped to pick it up, hoping they would ignore her and just walk by.

No such luck. Douglas's hand gripped her upper arm, helping her up. "Hello Taryn." The stony tone matched his expression.

"Oh! Hello. Sorry, I didn't see you." Taryn tried to act surprised.

"Have you met Carla? Carla, this is Taryn Christiansen,

the inn's new manager." He was acting the gentleman, but his eyes were thunderous.

"Hello Taryn." Carla matched Douglas's height, a head taller than Taryn, with perfectly made-up dark eyes, a beautiful tan, and long, straight chestnut hair pulled fashionably together at the nape of her neck. Her suit, a linen number in deep blue, looked custom-made. The woman exuded poise, confidence, expensive taste, and a no-nonsense attitude. She was beautiful—like a cold, untouchable, magazine model.

Taryn fought back a wave of self-consciousness, keeping her chin high and her back straight as she watched Carla briefly turn to Douglas, raise an elegantly arched brow, and direct an unspoken message his way. She faced Taryn again, extending a cool, strong, manicured hand. "How nice to meet you. You're not quite what I expected."

Taryn ignored the last remark, determined not to take any bait from a woman who, in the past few minutes, she had assessed as a barracuda. The thought of this woman as Douglas's fiancée was preposterous, so unfathomable that Taryn felt no jealousy whatsoever. They were completely mismatched, beside the fact that they would look good together on a magazine cover. She pulled up her trusty shield of professionalism, returning the handshake firmly, and met the unmasked curiosity in the woman's eyes with what she hoped was a confident smile. "A pleasure."

"If you'll excuse us," Douglas said to Carla, "Taryn and I have some business to discuss."

"Shall we add eavesdropping to your list of clandestine behaviors?" Douglas whispered accusingly the moment Carla made her way down the hall and into the saloon.

That stung. "I didn't hear a thing," Taryn lied, stooping quickly to pick up her pen. Upon straightening, her delicate gold necklace caught on one of her earrings.

"The hell you didn't." He paused, ran a hand through his hair in what seemed like frustration, then stared at her fingers as they tried to untangle the chain.

"I can't believe you and she were engaged," she blurted before she could stop herself.

Douglas looked down the hall to where Carla had disappeared. "Neither can I. She wasn't always . . ." he paused, "like that." He looked back at Taryn. "You're making it worse," he added, reaching over and gently attempting to untangle the chain from her earring. His mouth was pressed into a firm line, dark circles visible under his eyes.

He looked tired now, weary even. She wondered if he had slept as poorly as she had since their encounter by the lakeside. She closed her eyes to avoid looking into his. His scent filled her. She stopped herself from inhaling deeply. Thoughts of what could have been between them gently crept into her mind, but the memory of his more recent accusations quickly doused them. Why did he expect the worst of her? Because of what one woman had done to him?

The back of his hand brushed her cheek as he worked the chain loose. The contact, his nearness, hurt—each touch puncturing her heart like a tiny dagger.

"There," he said gruffly, dropping his hands, avoiding her gaze.

"Thank you." Taryn cleared her throat slightly. "I've got to check on Tina and Susan." The words rushed out and she all but ran down the hall. She thought she heard him say her name, but didn't look back. She couldn't look back.

Guests continued to file in for the ceremony, and Taryn spent the next few hours ushering them around, answering questions, directing staff, and constantly checking her lists. Every once in a while she had the odd sensation, evident by the raising of the tiny hairs on the back of her neck, that someone was watching her. The occasional quick look around revealed nothing, however, and she wrote it off to tension. There certainly was enough of that. Although everything was going well, she felt like she was walking among upright dominoes and that a slight misstep would start a chain reaction and ruin everything.

"Nice ceremony, didn't you think?" Aiden Randolf, wine-glass in hand and grinning proudly, later approached Taryn in the shade of the inn's wide porch.

"Wonderful, Aiden." Taryn smiled. He looked like he may have had more than just one glass of the rich red wine he carried, though he was far from drunk. The knot in his bow tie hung limply and he spoke slightly louder than necessary.

"Tremendous job you're doing here, Taryn." His arm made a wide, sweeping gesture, encompassing the inn and the grounds. "Just tremendous. Everything is ticking like clockwork. I hear business is picking up too. Good for you." He took a sip of his wine, glanced around at the other guests, and then gave her an earnest look. "We really regret losing you. We miss you at the hotel."

Taryn opened her mouth to speak, but Aiden's raised hand stopped her.

"No—don't explain. We've been through that, I know." He leaned towards her, conspiratorially. "Off the record?"

She gave a slight nod.

"Off the record, I realize that you were right. Todd was wrong for the job, but like I said before, my hands were tied. I'm so sorry you had to leave. He's gone now, you know. Moved up to head office by his uncle. Seems to be a whole different atmosphere now among the staff. I know you'd like it."

Taryn's heartbeat quickened. "What are you saying, exactly?" she asked quietly, too intent on what she thought Aiden might be suggesting to respond to the feeling that someone had just stepped up close behind her.

"I'm saying that the promotion is yours, if you choose to come back after your contract here is finished."

Taryn's heart leapt with joy. Her promotion! "That's wonderful, Aiden. Thank you."

Aiden grinned.

"Excuse me, Taryn." Douglas's voice was icy cool behind her. "Could I speak with you a moment?"

She froze. Could he not let her enjoy this one moment? "Excuse me, please, Aiden."

"Not at all, not at all. I know you're busy. We'll talk about this again," he said easily, already heading toward someone else on the porch.

Taryn whirled around to face Douglas and found herself confronting another of his stormy expressions.

"Eavesdropping?" she asked calmly.

"Making another deal?" he replied coldly.

It hit her like a ton of bricks—the realization that what Douglas had just overheard would confirm his suspicions of her. "That was not what you think it was," she said quickly.

"Wasn't it? It would seem to me that you're being rewarded for your work here with a promotion from your *other* employer. Congratulations."

"That's not exactly true."

"Then why don't you tell me what is true," he challenged.

Taryn refused to be falsely accused again. "I'm really getting sick of this." She faced him squarely, one hand on her hip, the other clutching her clipboard, and said in a steady, low voice, "I don't work for the Stanley Park Hotel or Hagen Enterprises. I left there when I didn't get the promotion I had worked for. I then got this job," she said, pointing at the floor, "but it ends at the end of September."

She paused for breath. The hum of happy conversation, clinking glasses, and soft music dimmed around them as they stared at each other. He said nothing, apparently waiting, his arms crossed over his chest. At least he was listening, she thought.

"I need to make a living after September. I've had no other offers. I now have an offer to return to the Stanley Park, as you've just overheard. The person who originally got the promotion—who happened to be Todd—has been transferred to head office. My former manager, Aiden Randolf, father of the bride, has now offered me the position Todd vacated, which should have been mine in the first place." She raised her chin. "Those are the facts, Douglas Prescott. I know you don't believe me, but that's the truth. If you'd rather believe that cock-and-bull story you relayed to me, there's nothing I can do about it."

Douglas leaned back against the bright, white porch railing, half his body in shade, half in bright sunlight. He seemed to be mulling over her words, his gaze moving over her face, but his expression remained hard.

"Taryn! Oh, my goodness." Margaret hastened toward them, breathless and flushed. "There's been a mix-up with the rooms. Can ye come, please?"

"That's actually what I had come to tell you," Douglas said, clicking back into business mode. "Sorry, Margaret. I got a bit distracted."

Taryn looked at him, wondering if what she'd said had any impact on him. She guessed not, by the look on his face. She turned and followed Margaret with a sigh.

No sooner had she assisted Margaret with the problem at the front desk than she spotted Tina signaling her from the door leading to the patio where the reception was about to start.

"The wine's going faster than expected," she said quietly when Taryn reached her, indicating the tray she held, heavily laden with glasses of both red and white wine. "Could you get someone to get more from the wine cellar?"

"No problem. I'll go." She needed a breather.

The wine cellar door opened off the hallway by the kitchen. Taryn paused on the stone steps, shutting the door behind her, letting her eyes adjust to the dim light after the brilliant sunshine outside. The cool, damp air, thick with the sweet, heavy, and slightly musty scent of wine, created a pleasant eruption of goosebumps on her skin. She inhaled deeply, thankful for a few minutes of relaxing quiet. She reached the bottom of the steps and walked along the bins, leaning in to find the wines the Randolfs preferred from the nearby Okanagan vineyards.

From the far end of the wine cellar she barely heard the door open and close at the top of the stairs. She looked up but couldn't see far enough up the stairs to see who it was. Fighting down a ridiculous sense of foreboding that welled up inside her, she felt the prickle of small hairs rising on the back of her neck. "Tina, is that you? Did you run out already? I'll be right there," she called.

No answer. She waited, watching the lower stairs. Expensive-looking men's shoes appeared first, then black designer trousers, then a crisp white dress shirt came into view as the intruder slowly descended the stairs. He reached the bottom and turned to face her with a wolf's smile.

Chapter Eleven

"You!" Taryn's fingers choked the bottle of Chablis she had just pulled out of a bin. "What the devil are you doing down here?"

"Gee, Taryn," Todd walked toward her, casually sliding his hands into his trouser pockets, "I'd hoped for a more hospitable welcome."

Taryn fought the urge to step back, raising her chin slightly. "I hope you're here to tell me you're going to fix this mess you've created." Her lips hardened and she shook her head slightly. "How could you do such a horrible thing?"

"I've been trying to find a chance to talk privately with you all day, to explain, to make you understand," he paused, then quietly added, "to make it right between us." His tone held a hint of malice.

Her stomach twisted. He wanted to make it right between them? She remembered the scene in the car. A seed of fear sprouted deep within her, replacing the indignation she'd felt at his arrival.

"After what you did? Not a chance." She busied her hands by replacing the Chablis and pulling out a Riesling from another bin, giving her cause to move a step away from him. Her gut instinct urged her out of the cellar. She pretended to

144

examine the label of the bottle she had just extracted, brushing off the dust with one hand.

He stepped closer. "This take-over business can work, Taryn, if you'll let it. It'll work for the inn, by ensuring some solid financial backing and consistent management. It'll work for Hagen, and it'll work for me. Do you have any idea what kind of promotion I'll get when I swing this, and the salary to go with it? Not to mention the finder's fee Uncle Elliot will hand me. And then I can make it all work for us too." He leaned against the bins and crossed his ankles. "I've always wished there could be more between us. You know that."

"Not interested Todd. I made that clear. And the inn will do much better without your intervention. Those are two things I'm positive about." His eyes, the intensity of that look . . . The passage was too narrow for her to step by him without being obvious.

"I've got to get some wine up to Susan and Tina." She began making her way farther along the bins, pulling bottles out, loading her arms as she went along, ignoring the marks the dusty bottles left on her dress. He walked behind her.

She reached the end of the passageway and turned, nearly bumping into him. "Oh!" She swallowed hard, trying not to show her growing anxiety. Her every movement felt exaggerated, unnatural, tense.

"Taryn, don't be this way. Look, I'm sorry about how this went down."

"Please let me by, Todd." Her breathing quickened. The stairs beckoned safety.

"You're just not listening, Taryn. This take-over is a great opportunity, really, best for everyone involved." Exasperation weighed his words, and his wide-legged stance effectively blocked her return along the passageway. "Will you just listen, for once?"

Taryn swallowed hard and looked past him, trying to decide how to get by.

He shook his head. "It's that night in the car, isn't it?" He frowned and shook his head, briefly massaging his forehead with two fingers. "Ah, Taryn, I'm sorry about that. I didn't mean to grab you like that, hold you. I just didn't want you running out into the night in the state you were in, didn't want you to leave mad."

"Forget it," she responded quickly. "I need to get going Todd."

"I've already started the process," he continued, switching back to his original topic, trying to hold her darting gaze with his. "The Thompson Trust take-over will happen without your help. But—"

"I don't understand what you want from me." She inched forward, prepared to make a dash past him.

"I might be able to arrange the foreclosure on the inn without your help too, but it sure would be quicker and easier if you cooperated. I'd make it worth your while."

"I'm not playing this game, Todd. The answer is no."

"Well, then remember the Staylander leak. I've already told you I've connected you to that. Sorry," he shrugged as she glared at him, "a man's got to take security measures. I can protect you or sink you if it all comes out—protect you if you cooperate. I don't make idle threats, Taryn. I hope you see that now. I need the money that bad."

"Are you deaf? The answer is no."

"I hear you've got a job lined up with Aiden this fall. I could arrange to have someone else in line for that position." He shrugged. "Or maybe not. I guess it depends on how cooperative you are in helping me solve my little problem."

Her jaw dropped at that. This whole business had already gone way beyond a grudge.

He laughed at her expression. "Oh, don't look so shocked. Of course I know about Aiden offering you that position. I'm privy to that kind of thing these days. Taryn, if you work with me on this, things could go so much better for you."

"No." She clung tightly to the bottles, and her principles.

She tried to step around him, but he blocked her way. She felt her cheeks flushing, rage building. "You're going to have to figure out another way. You're not taking over the inn if I have anything to say about it."

"Think about it, Taryn. Just let this place slide into a position where foreclosure would be easy, where we could buy it for a song—that shouldn't take much—and I'll arrange for you to get just about any job you want within Hagen Enterprises. You could even continue to run this dusty antique, if we keep it." He sniffed, his disdain obvious. "We could make some mutually beneficial arrangement, I'm sure."

She spoke slowly, distinctly. "The inn will make the payments and you'll have no opportunity to foreclose. End of story."

"That, my dear, would be a miracle." He pursed his lips; his eyes remained hard, cold, and calculating. "Too bad Prescott already thinks you're part of the plan. Funny how easily that took root. A shame, really." He reached toward her. "Why don't you let me help you with those bottles. They must be heavy."

She tried to step back but bumped into the wall. "Don't touch me."

"Oh, Taryn, for Pete's sake, I'm not going to hurt you." He spoke as though berating a child.

She turned her head and closed her eyes, then dropped the bottles against his body, jumping away as he started in surprise. At least one of them hit him squarely on the foot—she could tell by his yelp of pain. The rest shattered on the concrete floor, spraying wine and shards of glass in all directions.

She dashed past him, broken glass crunching under her feet, reaching the stairs before he recovered. But Todd was quick, and right behind her, muttering something about working it out. Clumsy in her haste, Taryn tripped up the steps. She tried to pull herself up by the railing. A scream rose in her throat, but she couldn't inhale deeply enough to push it out, a searing pain in her left side almost suffocating her.

A sudden shaft of bright light flooded the stairwell, accompanied by a crescendo of party noise from upstairs. Todd looked past her and rose, his expression flattening into strained innocence. Taryn pulled herself up a few more steps, wincing in pain at the effort. Though she had not yet turned around, and there was no sound of movement or words from behind her, she knew without a doubt who stood at the head of the stairs.

"What in the name of Hades is going on down here?" Douglas's voice boomed in the stairwell, his expression carrying all the fury of a thunderstorm. He eyed Taryn, who had brought herself to a standing position as she clung to the railing for support. "Bloody hell, Taryn." He took the few stairs separating them. "Are you bleeding? Look at your dress, your legs! Taryn, you're covered in blood. Sit down!" He pushed Taryn into a sitting position and glared at Todd, who stood at the bottom of the stairs trying to look nonchalant, wine stains covering his pants and splattered onto his white shirt.

"It's wine," Taryn said quickly, eyeing Todd, wondering what he would say. What a disaster!

"Wine?" Douglas looked them both over again. "It looks like you two slaughtered something down here!" His voice resonated with angry concern. He paused. The silence thickened. "I'm still waiting for an explanation." He directed his demand at Todd. His position on a higher step made him a towering and imposing figure—more so than usual. It was obvious no one was going anywhere.

"Douglas Prescott, meet Todd Hagen." Might as well throw the last of the gasoline onto the fire and be done with it, Taryn thought morosely.

"I know who he is. And I've been watching him watch you all day," Douglas said.

"We were getting more wine for the party and bumped into each other," Todd said quickly, his voice even, astounding Taryn with his apparent calm. "Taryn dropped hers and . . . they broke." He looked at Taryn, warning in his eyes.

"I see." But Douglas obviously did not see. He waited, his arms crossed, staring at Todd. "And that's it?"

Taryn opened her mouth to speak, and saw Todd's eyebrows rise in amused challenge. How would she put it, exactly? Angry, in pain, insulted, and frightened, Taryn was fed up with repeatedly trying to explain her behavior. She glanced at Todd as he went on.

"Taryn fell going up the stairs." Todd seemed to gain some confidence in the fact that Taryn hadn't said a word. "She was running for something to mop up the wine and glass. I was just going to help her up."

Douglas looked down at Taryn, searching her face. "Taryn?" He spoke quietly, seeking confirmation, but Taryn could see the anger in those stormy gray eyes. Anger, and something more. Suspicion. "What's going on?"

Scenarios shot like machine-gun fire in her mind's eye. Whatever he felt about her, whatever he believed, he would take any opportunity to have it out with Todd. And a score like that would not be settled in a verbal debate. Not with these two men. And then what? Physically, Todd wouldn't stand a chance. Although they were of similar height, Todd's physique was slighter, toned and trimmed at a gym. Taryn imagined the hard planes of Douglas's muscled frame, strength built from years of tough, physical work in the demanding environment of a ranch. No, Todd didn't stand a chance. But she was just as certain Todd would turn around and sue Douglas for assault, and likely the inn too. If worse came to worst, Douglas might even end up in jail. At the very least there would be legal fees to cover, far too many for the inn to sustain, given the situation. And then Todd would win anyway. He'd win everything. So there was that to consider as well. She had to ensure they didn't come to blows.

With gritty resolve Taryn forced a small smile to her lips and tried to keep her voice even. "I just dropped some bottles, then tripped up the steps. You know how accident-prone I am." She winced a bit, holding her side, as she got to her feet. "Now, let me get something to clean that up with," she said as she managed to squeeze by Douglas.

By the look on his face, Taryn could tell he didn't believe her for a moment.

She slipped back into the cellar not a minute later with mop, bucket, broom, and dust pan in hand, quickly closing the door behind her so as not to attract attention. She was instantly alarmed at the scene below her.

Douglas had Todd cornered on the lower landing. Eye to eye, mere inches apart, Todd was barely visible behind Douglas's broad frame. Douglas's fists were clenched at his sides, his arms and shoulders tense, but he made no move to strike. Taryn held her breath, rooted to the step.

". . . and I don't want to hear about Taryn dropping any more bottles, or tripping up steps, or even stubbing her toe if she's anywhere near you." The words grated, the threat behind them clear as the water in Aspen Lake. "Understood?"

"Step aside, Prescott." Todd all but spat at him, but made no move, his dour expression set in concrete. He was mean, but not stupid.

Douglas slowly moved aside, relaxing his fists, gesturing up the stairs with one arm.

Taryn slowly made her way down the stairs with her supplies, passing Todd on his way up. Aside from turning himself sideways as he passed her, he made no acknowledgement of her presence, then clicked the door shut without a backward glance.

"Are you alright?" Douglas's tone was less than doting.

"Fine." She stepped by him, avoiding his eyes, and made her way toward the disaster area. Douglas followed slowly.

"So, what, exactly, was going on down here?"

Taryn kept her head down, picking up the larger chunks of glass with shaking hands, dropping them into the bucket he held for her. Her nerves were raw. She had been pushed to her limit. "What did Todd tell you?"

"I want you to tell me," he said firmly. "I've never seen two people look more guilty."

It was going to be Todd's word against hers. Again. Taryn paused at her task, but didn't look up.

"Taryn, I want to know what is going on between the two of you. No, the three of you—you and Todd and Hagen Enterprises. The future of this inn, of this community, is at stake, and I'm through messing around with uncertainties."

He put the bucket down with a heavy clunk, pulling her upright by her elbow. She wrenched it from him. "I've already told you." Her side ached, her knees were bruising from her fall on the stairs, her insides still shook from the frightening exchange with Todd . . . And now this inquisition! She didn't know how much more she could take. She searched his stony expression. A memory of times when his features were gentler, more loving, flashed through her mind. A week ago he'd have taken this chance meeting in the wine cellar to kiss her, as part of the game he'd made of her compromise. And what a wonderful game that had become, she now admitted. She wanted him to hold her now, tight and safe against his body. She wanted him to trust her. She needed his strength. Not more suspicion, more questions, more demands. The dense oaf. Couldn't he see that?

"You don't believe me anyway. So just let me do my job and leave me be." She bent again toward the broken glass on the floor.

"What am I supposed to think when I come into the wine

cellar and see the two of you horsing around, Taryn?" He dragged his hand through his hair with a deep breath. "Every time I turn around you seem to be doing something else that looks suspicious, given the information I received from Thompson Trust." He paused, taking a few steps down the passageway with his hands on his hips, then spun on his heel to face her again. "How do you think that makes me feel? I wanted to believe in you, but you didn't make it easy. And you're not making it any easier today."

"It's only suspicious because you have such a untrusting nature," Taryn argued, anxious to lash out. "I'm just doing what I was hired to do!"

"You came from Hagen, you're going back to Hagen. They've bought our credit company and they're after this property now. Help me out here."

"Do you have any idea how insulting that is? My motivation—you paranoid, overbearing, control-monger—is to fulfil the terms of my contract and move on to another job with an excellent employment reference that will propel my career!" *This is pointless,* Taryn told herself. "Look. I am not Carla, so don't let your past problems—"

"Don't you dare bring her into this." Douglas stepped closer, the grays of his eyes almost black with anger. "She's got nothing to do with it."

Once the claw was sunk, Taryn couldn't resist the urge to give it a tug. "Maybe you should think about that some more before you deny it so vigorously. Maybe you can't trust me because she betrayed you." Taryn couldn't stop herself from one more dig. "Don't make me suffer for your past errors in judgement."

"And what the hell would you know about it anyway?" Douglas fumed. He grabbed her elbow as she bent again to clean up the glass, keeping her on her feet, facing him. "There's way too much at stake here for me to be passive—"

"Passive? You? Ha!"

His eyes narrowed. A muscle ticked along his jaw line as his gaze raked her face, pausing at her lips. A little voice inside her whispered a warning. Her coiled nerves tightened as the silence thickened.

"That sharp tongue of yours is going to get you into a lot of trouble one day." He pulled her into a brittle embrace. The breath rushed out of her like a popped balloon.

"Listen Taryn," he ground out quietly, his lips so close to hers she could feel his breath fanning them. "Whatever your motivation, you do good work. It's one reason you're still here. Another is the fact that I can't seem to get enough of you, and I'll tell you plainly that it disturbs me. You'd think I would have learned the first time."

Taryn pushed against him. He released her.

"My personal weaknesses aside," he continued, "you have considerable evidence stacked up against you, circumstantial though it may be, and I need to protect the only things in my life that matter: my home, family, and community. But I wouldn't expect someone with a life like yours to understand that."

Taryn's eyes widened in shock as she absorbed his cold-hearted attack. What kind of callous swine would insult a person's lack of real home or family? The truth of it had been a painful emptiness growing within her ever since she arrived in this beautiful place. To have it thrown in her face like that was beyond cruel. Tears welled in her eyes. She bit the inside of her lip to hold them in. She'd sooner die than have him see her cry.

Frustration overwhelmed her. She raised her hand to slap him. He grabbed it quickly with his free hand, held it for a moment to prove he could, then pushed it back to her side and released it.

"That's becoming a bad habit of yours. Slapping me isn't going to change things, Taryn."

"I hate you."

He smiled grimly, releasing her completely. "And that just makes wanting me to hold you all the more infuriating, doesn't it?"

"You're delusional."

He trapped her gaze with his. They must have stood there for a full minute, shooting silent sparks at one another, a hand's breadth apart, lips grim, jaws tight. A stand-off.

He exhaled hard, as if he'd been holding his breath too long. "Taryn, what the hell are we doing?"

"I don't know what *you're* doing. *I'm* just trying to protect myself," she whispered, still fighting back tears.

He shook his head slightly. "You don't ever need to protect yourself from me." He pressed her gently back against the cool concrete wall. Before she knew what was happening, he kissed her, gently, sending curls of warmth through her core. Her small inner voice, shouting rational thoughts, struggled to be heard. She tried to focus on it, to call it back, but it was no use.

He ended the kiss abruptly, pulling away with such force that she leaned forward as he leaned back, momentarily off balance. She shook her head, trying to clear her mind.

"No delusion there," he said with quiet satisfaction.

Her heart snapped with the realization that she'd been played again. "You're such an arrogant brute." She shoved away from him and made for the stairs.

"Taryn." The word rang sharp, intense. "I didn't mean it like that. Taryn!" He closed the distance between them and took her hand. She tried to pull it away, but he held fast. "We haven't solved anything."

"No, we haven't," she responded coldly.

"This isn't turning out as I'd hoped."

'This' could mean a lot of things. "It's a disaster." The response applied, regardless.

His expression turned serious. "Marry me."

"What?" she shouted in disbelief, ripping her hand from his. Her hair must have stood on end. "Are you *crazy?*"

"Marry me," he repeated.

She stared at him, her mind racing, and then it hit her. What a tidy solution. She began to fume. If she married him, she'd become "trustworthy." That's what this was all about, wasn't it? As his wife, she couldn't possibly let Hagen take over the inn, because she would have an obvious vested interest. And he'd have a built-in manager for the inn, someone who could keep it profitable.

The seconds ticked by. He continued to wait, watching her intently, as if he knew the brilliance of the idea would dawn on her eventually. The more she thought of it, the more it crushed her. Why would he think she'd consider marrying him? Did he know she was in love with him? Would he be so heartless as to take advantage of that weakness?

She couldn't believe how things had gotten so bad so fast. Yes, she still loved him. She couldn't understand it, even refused to accept it. She'd spat words of hate at him, but the love was there anyway. Love was the strangest of emotions, she reflected. More than an emotion, love was a being, a separate entity, sometimes sprouting to life in the oddest places. It had sprung up in the energy that flowed between herself and Douglas, and settled itself in her unwilling heart. She thought fleetingly of the bright, tiny flowers that grew in tiny cracks on sheer rock faces. Unlikely, but there they were.

And this proposal? On his part a loveless marriage? Was this what Carla had done to him? Cheapened the sacred institution of marriage into a business negotiation? Shock gave way to pain and her throat began to constrict on the hard lump forming there. Without another word, she turned to go.

Taryn had reached the first step as his hand gently gripped her shoulder, turning her to face him. "I don't make the proposal lightly. You could at least do me the honor of giving a reply." Her departure made the answer obvious, of course, but he forced her to face him with it anyway.

She swallowed a few times, trying to control her emotions, praying her voice wouldn't crack. "I realize it must have cost you a great deal to ask someone like me to marry you," she whispered with trembling lips, "someone with a life history like mine, someone you don't trust, don't respect, and therefore cannot love." She searched his face for a crack in the cold, closed expression. Nothing. "You might want to think about what that says about you, nevermind me. And you're probably just as concerned about my saying yes and being stuck with me, as you are with my saying no and having your doubts about me continue to fester. But, knowing what you think of me and what motivated your proposal, a reply to it would give it a dignity it doesn't deserve."

He watched her quietly for a moment, his jaw tightening. "Well, that was a fine little speech." He paused. "And just how the hell do you know what motivated my proposal?" The words came slowly. His grip on her shoulder stiffened, but there was a part of her that knew not to be afraid of him. Physically, at least, Douglas would never hurt her.

"Marriage should be for love, based on mutual respect and trust," she whispered, "not a strange combination of business and . . ."

"Damn it! What do you want from me?" He forced the words out, obviously fighting for control.

She just stared at him, her whole being completely shattered. *Love, trust, and respect. It's not something you get by asking. It needs to be given freely,* her heart answered.

"What?" he repeated fiercely, the word piercing the silence.

She slowly pulled his hand off her shoulder. "I have to go."

"Go then," he said, in a voice so low she could hardly hear it. "And don't look back, Taryn."

The morning sun streamed through the white lace curtains of the coffee shop, creating dappled patterns over the crisp, pale blue linen tablecloths. Its warmth already penetrated the slight morning chill that hung in the air as summer faded into an early autumn. Still half asleep after another restless night, Taryn paused as she entered, inhaling the aromas of Gertrude's fresh baking—muffins, cinnamon buns, bread.

The pleasant assault on her senses was only a temporary salve, however, for the hollow feeling that had remained with her since the scene in the wine cellar. Todd was gone, thank goodness. And she had seen Douglas briefly on only three occasions since then. Avoiding eye contact, their exchanges were short, tense, and strictly business. By the third encounter, without saying as much, they seemed to have realized an uneasy but stable truce. It allowed her to breathe at least a little easier, though her nerves were still on edge whenever he was near.

"There she is!" someone said loudly as others started applauding. It was Gordon, sitting at one of the corner tables with Margaret, Susan, and Tina. He raised his coffee cup to her in a toast. "Congratulations, Taryn! Well done!"

Taryn forced a smile and walked in. The others raised their cups as well, beaming. She blushed as she leaned over the counter to pour herself a coffee. "Congratulations should go to all of you," she insisted, pulling up a chair to join them. "It did go well, didn't it?"

The guests had begun their exodus the previous day, all smiles and pleasantries. By evening the clean-up was almost done.

Gordon leaned over and presented her with a pink rose, and she accepted it with a broad smile. "It's gorgeous, thank you Gordon." Taryn inhaled the pale flower's delicate fragrance. "Oh, and I never did thank you for the one you left on my desk one morning a few weeks back." She laughed. "I don't think I've even seen you for more than a few seconds since then, we've all been so busy."

"It was perfect," Tina said dreamily, "story-book perfect. Did you see the bride and groom? Oh gosh, she was so pretty and he was so gorgeous and they were so in love . . ." She slumped back in her chair and sighed.

Susan elbowed her playfully. "Listen to Cinderella here."

Taryn saw Margaret and Gordon exchange small, private smiles. To have a love like that, Taryn thought. One that changed and grew over the years. Now that would be storybook perfect.

Gordon turned his attention back to Taryn. "You're welcome, I think, but I don't remember giving you a rose before now. Marg here keeps me on a short leash." He gave a mock grunt as Margaret nudged him. "Are you sure you didn't steal one?" he teased.

"No, Gordon, I wouldn't steal your roses. But there was one on my desk a few weeks ago, I remember quite distinctly." And she did. It was the morning after Douglas had walked out on her. The morning he'd taken off into the hills for days on end instead of trying to mend the rift between them.

"Douglas did it," Susan chimed in, taking a big bite of her muffin.

"Did what?" a deep, honey-smooth voice said from right behind Taryn, making her spine tingle.

"Stole a rose, it seems," Tina answered, her interest piqued.

"Never." Douglas filled his coffee cup and squeezed in between Taryn and Margaret. Taryn felt the full length of his thigh as it pressed against hers. The sensation tripped her thoughts momentarily, and she took a slow sip of coffee to maintain her composure.

"Took one with permission," Gordon corrected. "I remember now."

The significance of Douglas leaving her a rose the morning after their argument was slowly taking shape in Taryn's mind. It had been a secret acknowledgement, she suddenly realized. A tender, silent indication of his feelings. In his own subtle way, he'd let her know he was thinking of her even as he felt compelled to give each of them some time and space to deal with what was happening between them.

"Oh yes, I remember," Margaret looked thoughtful. "He put it on your desk one morning a while back."

Douglas seemed surprised and looked at Taryn, one brow raised in puzzlement. "I thought you didn't want anyone to know about us," he challenged with both brows now raised.

"They don't," Taryn replied through clenched teeth, trying to cast him a subtle 'shut-up' glance, which was nearly impossible as all eyes were now on her. "And there's nothing to know."

"Oh, for the love of Pete," Margaret admonished. "The secret's out, and it's about time, I'd say. The two of ye have been dancing around each other like overcharged fireflies since Taryn got here." She frowned at Douglas. "You, young man . . . I was pained at seeing ye so gun-shy after Carla, it's about time ye came around, and a nicer lass ye'll never find, mark me words."

"Ah, Margaret—" Douglas's tone held an exasperated weariness.

Taryn could feel her cheeks burning and wanted to slide under the table. "There's no 'us,' " she said before Margaret went on.

"Now Taryn, love, how can ye say that? Just look at the two of ye. Don't worry, we'll no be makin' a fuss over it now. Just wanted to say me piece, now that the secret's out."

Now even Douglas looked uncomfortable. "There's nothing going on. Really."

Taryn stared into her coffee cup and said nothing more.

"Oh . . ." Margaret suddenly seemed taken aback. "Is that so then? I see." An awkward silence fell over the table.

"Hey! There you all are!" Alison exploded into the coffee shop, waving a newspaper. "Have you seen this?" She smacked the paper down in the middle of the table, obviously unaware that she'd just sliced through tension a foot thick.

Taryn peered over, examining the article Alison had circled, more than happy to divert the attention away from herself.

"It's the *Vancouver Tribune's* social column. We got coverage! Good coverage, Taryn! Look!" Alison leaned over between Douglas and Margaret, giving Douglas a slight nudge. "Make room for the pregnant lady, Dougie." She sent him leaning further into Taryn. He put an arm on the back of Taryn's chair as Taryn tried to shrink away, uncomfortable with the contact.

"Look, it says right here, 'and the couple tied the knot at the gloriously romantic Aspen Creek Inn, a superb oasis of frontier Victoriana just outside of Kamlen.' And . . ." Alison flipped over to the travel section where a small photo of the inn topped a short article hailing it as one of Vancouver's best-kept getaway secrets. Alison rattled off the high points of the article, concluding with, "It's perfect!"

It was fabulous news. The table suddenly buzzed with excited chatter. Taryn felt immensely pleased, though the earlier discussion dampened her joy. "That's probably why we've had more calls than usual this morning," she said, tucking the rose behind her ear. The soft jingle of another incoming call gave her an excuse to make her exit. "Great job, everyone. Excuse me, I'd better get that one."

A few minutes of star-gazing, then to bed, Taryn told herself as she packed up the last of her paperwork and headed out onto the porch. Her contract was done. Every indication was that they'd broken even for the season. The best in a decade. She'd never worked so hard in all her life. Tomorrow there'd be a small party to celebrate their success. Then back to Vancouver for her. She let the screen door bounce shut behind her. The inn was closed. No guests to disturb. The cool night air revived her senses. The porch swing creaked slightly on its hinges as she set it in motion, leaning her head back against the soft cotton cushion.

The night was quiet, peaceful, perfect. A blissful sigh escaped her, then her thoughts immediately turned to Douglas. She couldn't help it. It happened every time her mind was idle, sometimes even when it wasn't. She'd seen little of him in the three weeks since the incident in the wine cellar. Just a few brief, business-like exchanges as the season wound down. He did his work; she did hers. The tension remained between them, strung tight as a bow. The ache in her heart remained too, dull and deep, carving its own little hollow as if intending to stay.

"Sleeping out here tonight?" Douglas's voice came from the doorway.

Taryn's head jerked up. How did he always manage to surprise her like that?

"I thought you had to go back to the cows, or the horses, or whatever," she stammered, hating herself for her loss of composure. "Get ready for the round up, I mean." She knew they were soon bringing the cattle down for the winter.

"Thought you may need some help tying up loose ends here." He leaned against the railing and gave the swing a gentle push with his foot, setting it in motion again. Taryn hadn't noticed it'd stopped.

She looked out into the night. Stars filled the sky here. In Vancouver, she'd only ever seen a few scattered about. The brightest ones, people said. But out here, without the lights of the city, there were millions. It amazed her. "Oh." She paused. "No need, thanks. There's only a few things left. I can finish that off in the morning."

Silence. Her hand tightened on the swing's chain, the metal links cool in her palm.

He shifted slightly. "Fine then." He paused. "I also wanted to thank you."

She looked away. "Don't mention it."

"I mean it. You saved our hides this season. We'll manage with the payments for now. I don't think Hagen'll be able to take us."

The words held an uncomfortable formality. After everything they'd been through, did it all came down to this?

"I'm glad." And she was. But then why did she feel like crying? "I'm really glad it worked out."

"So you're off tomorrow then? The new job?"

She nodded. "Starts next week. I've been looking for a place to live. Need to check out a few apartments, get moved in." They were talking about the wrong thing. She didn't want to talk about leaving. She was suddenly unable to trust her voice.

He nodded. "I can't make it to the party."

She raised her hand briefly, to indicate that she wasn't concerned about his absence. She thought she saw the Big Dipper in the sky, but wasn't sure. She squinted up at it. The stars began to run together.

He rose then. "Well, thanks again Taryn. Have a safe trip." He gave the swing another gentle push and stepped off the porch, into the night.

The next day, Taryn pulled away from the inn, a smile glued to her trembling lips, and waved at the small group that had become her summer family. A hollowness gnawed at her stomach, tears welled in her eyes. At the end of the driveway she allowed herself one look in the rear-view mirror. Through the thin haze of dust kicked up by the car's wheels, she saw that almost everyone had begun to disperse. But Douglas remained as before, leaning against the fence on his elbows, watching her go. It was then that she finally let the tears slide down her cheeks with abandon.

Chapter Twelve

Taryn stared at the manila envelope on her desk. "Douglas Prescott, Aspen Creek Ranch," the return address read. The courier had delivered it yesterday. She'd picked it up three or four times already, then dropped it and returned to the stacks of reports screaming their approaching deadlines at her.

It's just your check and some leftover paperwork. Leave it for the moment. The truth was, she wasn't sure how many more memories she could take right now.

Just this morning she'd seen a bouquet of pink roses in the hotel lobby, being delivered to some fortunate guest. They brought on a pang of yearning, hollowing her stomach. Her memories of Aspen Creek, never far from her mind, had tangled themselves into her every thought since then, making concentration difficult.

Gordon's roses. Pink climbers, most of them. Not the icy perfect, scentless, greenhouse variety she'd seen today. No, her memory flooded with scrambling branches and aromatic blossoms rioting uninhibited in the country sunshine. She remembered them gleaming in the night too, catching the glow from the *aurora borealis* as Douglas carted her out onto the porch and shared heaven's art with her. She remembered their scent wafting up onto the porch as she sipped iced tea with Alison, and later with Douglas . . .

There were many times in the past few weeks that she'd found herself staring out her office window at the spectacular Vancouver view. But the mountains rising on the other side of the inlet, the boats bobbing on the water, and the sun sparkling off the other high-rises of the downtown core just didn't provide the satisfaction they once did. Instead, her mind's eye constantly conjured up the view from a different window. It was tall and narrow with Victorian lace curtains that billowed in the breeze off the dark blue waters of Aspen Lake. Her window. Her room.

She knew now what that pang of yearning was. The pink roses had made her feel homesick. The realization brought a certain exhilaration, abating the hollowness somewhat. *Homesick.* She'd never felt it before. It meant, in her own mind at least, that she'd left some roots there at Aspen Creek. *Taryn Christiansen. Homesick.* She smiled to herself. *Taryn Christiansen wants to go home.*

She'd just, in the last hour, resolved to speak with Fred about renewing her contract at the inn for next season. She was also ready to pitch Fred a proposal for a winter opening, from Christmas to Valentine's Day, as Alison had suggested. The decision, once made, both excited and humbled her. As far as she knew, he hadn't yet made any arrangements to replace her. She heard from Alison that Fred's semi-retirement had lasted about two weeks, after which the weather turned foul, the golf course closed, and he claimed with a laugh that he needed more to do.

As for Douglas, Alison said she'd seen very little of him since the inn closed. If Taryn did return, she and Douglas would have to maintain some kind of peaceful co-existence. She drummed her fingers on the stack of paper in front of her.

She'd told him she hated him. At the time she believed it; his hurtful words had sliced into her that deeply. But she knew it wasn't the truth. What she hated was his power to make her forget the tidy rules she'd developed to protect herself from uncomfortable feelings. And where did that power come from? She gave it to him, morose as it sounded.

But those feelings weren't so uncomfortable anymore, she realized. She reached for the envelope again, turning it over in her hands. *When had it all changed? And how could it have all changed so quickly?* She had only been at the inn for a couple of months. It had affected her, drastically altering her views on some of the issues that were important in her life—like falling in love at, as her mother would advise, the wrong time in her career. But she loved Douglas.

She simply had to accept it now, regardless of the timing. It was some kind of chemistry, a mysterious magnetism that drew her to him, an instinct. She remembered every moment they'd shared. Everything was intensified with Douglas— her senses, emotions, observations. She laughed harder, and cried harder; saw beauty sooner and longer. She noticed and appreciated more of life's little things. Regardless of their differences, she felt more complete with him than she had at any other time in her life.

Conceding that, and knowing he did not love her, could she still go back to Aspen Creek? She spun her chair around and stared out the window. The answer was yes. Her brief stay at Aspen Creek had also altered her view on roots. Now that she'd had a taste of being in a place that felt like home, she needed more. Living in Aspen Creek—and, admittedly, having Douglas in her life there was a key part of that— made her realize how important and satisfying having a home and roots could be. She wanted to be part of the Aspen Creek community. She'd be near Alison and watch her best friend's baby grow up. She'd have Gordon teach her about the local plants and wildlife, in his quiet, fatherly way. And she'd revel in and absorb Margaret's motherly nature. One day, she thought to herself, she might actually have a real conversation with the shy, tight-lipped Barrel. She'd be there on the day Hans and Gertrude finally stopped bickering and admitted they were in love. And, through it all, she'd be near Douglas.

Taryn sighed. Perhaps seeing Douglas there occasionally would be enough to soothe her heart. Perhaps, she dared hope, after a time, they could give their relationship another try. Her desire to return to Aspen Creek was strong enough for her to make the necessary sacrifices; to take on whatever emotional challenges her return posed. If she didn't try now, she knew she'd regret it for the rest of her life. Of course, her career was still critical. She couldn't let go of that. But could there be a more satisfying career challenge than making the inn successful, knowing how important it was to the community?

A knock at the door spun her around. "Come in!" Aiden popped his head in, eyebrows raised in silent question. She laughed. "No. No baby news from Alison yet. Any time now." She gestured with her arm. "Please, come in. You're going to make the most doting grandfather once your own daughter decides to have children, Aiden. It is sweet that you have been so concerned about Alison."

"I have some news for you, actually," he said as he entered, closing the door behind him. "Wanted you to hear it from me before the rumor mills turn it inside out."

She waited for him to sit. "Not bad news I hope."

"No," he said with a smile. "Todd's been fired." He twirled his hands like a side-show magician.

She blinked a few times as her jaw dropped, and barely stopped herself from stupidly repeating the words as a question. "How? Why?" she asked, once she found her voice.

"Turns out he was the leak to Staylander about the Galiano Island property." He shook his head. "Can you believe it?"

"Oh, my . . ." Fear tightened Taryn's throat. "How did it come about?"

"Came from the legal department, is all I heard. Elliot called him in right away to ask him about it. Apparently he confessed then. That's all I know." He sat back in his chair. "I'm sure there was more to it than that, but it's a family matter as well as a business matter, so maybe we'll never know."

Did Carla do something? Taryn shook her head, wanting to know more but wondering how many questions would sound suspicious. Did Todd implicate her in any way, as he'd threatened to do? "When did it happen?"

"Yesterday."

No one had called her, that was a good sign. Maybe Todd hadn't even tried to drag her into it. Her fear began to ebb a bit. She pulled her shoulders down, trying to drive the tension out of them. "And he was out the door, just like that?"

Aiden snapped his fingers. "Just like that. His secretary was asked to box his personal items from his office and courier them to his home." Aiden rose to leave. "Just between you and me, I've never liked the man."

Her phone rang and she reached to answer it, nodding at Aiden as he made his way out. The sound of Margaret's voice caused her to sit up straight in her chair. "Aiden, wait." She signaled to him with her hand.

"Taryn, love, I'm calling to let ye know ye've become an honorary auntie." The laughter in her voice was infectious. Taryn's heart jumped with joy, pushing a giggle out of her. Aiden smiled from the doorway.

"And you, then, an honorary grannie! Margaret, what is it? Boy or girl?"

"A wee laddie, healthy and kickin', and in a big hurry to come into the world, he was. There was no time to call ye, lass. An easy time she had of it, God be praised. Alison sends her love. She desperately wants to see ye. Can ye come?"

Taryn glanced at Aiden, raising her brows. He guessed her

question and made shooing motions with his hands. "I'll be there tomorrow," she said into the receiver.

Aiden hovered in the doorway as Taryn said her good-byes. "Good thing it's Thursday. I'll only be gone over the weekend."

"Take all the time you need." He sighed as he went out the door. "A new baby. What a wonder."

Taryn felt buoyant enough now to face Douglas's envelope. She tore it open. Something fell out and dropped onto her lap, causing her to jump. She stared at it in surprise, then gingerly picked it up, tears suddenly pricking her eyes. A pink rose, neatly dried and pressed. She bit her lip, emotion swelling within her, forming a lump in her throat. She placed the rose on her desk and pulled the papers out of the envelope, absently unfolding them for a quick scan. And a scan was all it took. She gasped and jumped out of her chair, shooting it back against the wall. The papers floated to the floor in front of her, released from hands suddenly afraid to touch them. A yellow note caught her eye. She read it off the floor, recognizing Douglas's bold, vertical printing: *Alison said you'd visit once her baby was born. Please stop by and see me about this. Douglas.*

Taryn must have stood there for a full minute, just staring at the papers on the floor, before collecting herself and stooping to put them back in order. She stuffed the papers and, more carefully, the dried rose back into the envelope, turned off her computer, and grabbed her briefcase. "That man has some explaining to do," she muttered under her breath as she headed out the door.

She knew the road to the inn well enough, having driven it a few times during her stay. But night driving was a bit disorienting, just the same. The turnoff to Douglas's home was just up ahead, she remembered, squinting into the darkness.

Suddenly an animal hobbled through her car's headlight

beams, dragging its hind leg. Taryn skidded to a stop. It looked like Chip. She got out of her car.

"Chip!" she called, peering at the bushes into which the animal had disappeared. She heard a rustle and called again.

"Chip!" The dog slowly limped toward her. In the headlight's glow she could see his hind leg was covered in blood. Knowing not to grab at an injured dog, she crouched on the ground, gently calling him to her. He came slowly, and gave her hand a quick sniff-test. Within moments she had him in the back seat of her car. She didn't care about the bloodstains; the poor dog was suffering.

She started driving again, making what she hoped were comforting noises to Chip, who lay quietly behind her. *Oh God, don't let him die,* she silently pleaded. At the turnoff to Douglas's home she suddenly wondered if he'd be there. No matter, she thought, veering onto the rough gravel track. If necessary, she'd break a window and use his phone.

Relief at seeing the light glowing in the window sent her breath out in a rush. She rolled to a stop and jumped out of the car, stumbling slightly on the uneven ground in her haste. She ran up the stairs just as the door opened, flooding the porch with light.

"Taryn? What on earth . . . Are you okay?" He moved toward her, confusion clouding his expression as his gaze gathered her in. "Is that blood? What's wrong—"

"In the car," she breathlessly cut him off. "It's Chip. He's hurt."

"Go on inside," he said over his shoulder. He was back in a moment, Chip in his arms, the dog's blood on his shirt and hands. He lay Chip down on the braided rug in front of the fireplace and dragged the lamp closer. "Stay, boy," he commanded when the dog tried to rise. "Lie down. Stay." Chip's tail thumped a bit on the rug, and Taryn took that as a good sign. She knelt beside Chip, stroking his head as Douglas retrieved a first aid kit and began his ministrations.

Within moments, bloodied gauze littered the floor around them as Douglas cleaned the wound. "Thanks for coming, Taryn," he said without looking up, taking a clean piece of gauze from her hand. "Can you pass me that bottle there?"

"Here, this one?"

"Yes, take the cap off, will you, love? It's disinfectant."

She did as he asked. "You dropped quite a bombshell with that envelope. I had to come."

"Looks like he got tangled up in some barbed wire. It's messy, but he'll be okay." He glanced at her. "If you hadn't come, I would have dropped in on you next week." He gestured with his chin. "Scissors? I need to cut this fur away."

She passed him the scissors, and more gauze, then scratched Chip lightly behind the ears. "Is that why there's two suitcases and a gorgeous suit hanging at the bottom of the stairs over there?" She'd noticed them when she came in, wondering where he was going, fighting a sudden wave of alarm at the thought of his leaving.

He looked up suddenly, knocking his head into hers with a solid 'thunk.'

"Owww! Sorry," they said in unison.

"Partly," he answered. "Can you find the painkillers in there? They're pills."

"Crimey, you've got a hard head," she said, rubbing her own, enjoying the small smile that turned the edges of his mouth. She selected two bottles and held them out for him to identify.

He nodded at one then said, "I've got meetings set up with bankers, and a lawyer or two, to see about re-financing the loan on the inn. Now that we can meet our payment schedule with Hagen, I thought it best we cut and run to a more—shall we say—objective financial backer."

"Now there's an idea." So, he would have come to see her? The thought warmed her heart.

He began wrapping the wound in the bandage she'd pulled out of the kit. "It's not as bad as it looks, though he'll need stitches, and some antibiotics, I think. I'll call the vet. He's on rounds this evening, likely still at the MacGregors." He leaned closer to Chip's head as the dog tried to rise. "No, stay," he commanded, then popped a pill into Chip's mouth and clamped the dog's jaw shut until he swallowed. Chip slumped back down, eyes huge and pained, watching his master.

With one hand on Chip's head, Douglas turned to Taryn. "You're quite an assistant. You've done this before?"

"Never."

His eyebrows went up at that. "Oh. Well, I shouldn't be surprised. You seem competent at whatever you tackle. It seems we make a good team." He bent to clean up.

She didn't comment, but let the compliment settle within her as she helped him. When they'd finished she looked at his clothes, then at her own. "We look like butchers. I'm going to the car to get my purse and a clean blouse."

He pointed to a bathroom beside the entrance. "You can change in there." He caught her eye and paused. "Really, thanks for coming. And thanks for bringing him."

When she returned, Douglas had changed too, and was already in the kitchen at the far end of the huge room. It was an open floor plan, with living, dining and kitchen areas surrounding a big, stone fireplace in the center. She glanced around, taking it all in. Cedar paneling, exquisite hardwood floors, thick throw rugs, all in earth tones—dark green, brown, tan, gold, and russet. It suited him.

Taryn sat on the sofa and bent to give Chip a reassuring pat. "Lie still, boy." Chip thumped his tail again and gave a sigh, laying his head on the rug.

"How have you been?" he said from the kitchen, his back to her. His voice took on that characteristic smooth, mesmerizing quality she remembered so well. She had forgotten the effect it had on her. It stroked her senses like a feather on bare skin. "I was going to—" The rest of his words were cut off by the crash of an ice tray. He turned then and came back to the sofa with two glasses of juice. He handed her one, eyes intent, apparently awaiting her answer.

"Thanks," she murmured, then looked away, her gaze unable to hold his. What could she say? Homesick? Lonely? Tired? Stressed? Depressed? He'd laugh. "Really, really busy with the new job," she replied vaguely as he took a seat on the chair, Chip between them.

They looked at each other in silence for a few moments, and Taryn felt an awkwardness settle into the room now that the urgency of Chip's injury had abated. Douglas was just as handsome as she remembered him. More so, even. She drank in his features as he bent again to stroke Chip. Soft flannel shirt and his usual faded Levi's. He needed to shave, she thought, noting the stubble darkening his jaw. Or, rather, he didn't. Unshaven was just fine too—she stopped herself short. *Better get right to this . . .* She bent and retrieved the envelope from her purse. "This is probably a good time to talk about this, if you don't mind." She slid it across the end table to him.

He stared at it for a moment, as if debating whether or not to pick it up, or discuss it. He nodded gravely, then took it. She watched him shake the contents out. He caught the rose first, eyed it carefully, then picked the papers up from his lap. Taryn thought she saw his hand tremble. Was he nervous? It seemed so foreign a concept when applied to this man. She waited.

Douglas moved to sit on the sofa beside her, his smooth confidence apparently restored. Perhaps the tremor in his hand was just her imagination, she told herself, watching him.

"This," he said, "is supposed to show you how much I've missed you." He held the rose out to her, placing it gently in her palm as she opened her hand. "And to remind you of . . . well, here, this place." He gave her a crooked smile.

Her heart-rate doubled.

"This," he laid the papers on her lap, "is supposed to show

you how much I trust you. I'm hoping it'll make up for the lack of trust I showed before, when you were here."

She looked down at the papers, then back at him. "Douglas, what are you talking about?"

"I thought if I trusted you with something you knew was extremely important to me, a huge part of my life and my home, then you'd forgive me for . . . before."

"Douglas, isn't this a little extreme? It's the deed for the inn, for heaven's sake!"

He gave his head a quick shake. "It's yours. Just take over the loan payments. Run it like you've done this past season and you won't have any trouble gaining clear title in a few years. Fred agreed. It's mine to give, actually. I'm Fred's heir. I talked it over with him. We both know you've done more with the inn in the short time you were here than anyone has done in a decade, at least. You put your heart into it—against the odds, I might add."

"I simply can't accept it. Douglas, this," she shook the papers, "is probably worth a fortune!"

He smiled and shrugged.

"Well." She was flabbergasted. "Why has it become so important for you to prove that you trust me?" She didn't want to sound bitter, but the words came out almost of their own accord. "I really could have used your trust about a month or so ago."

"I'm sorry." He paused as if searching for words. "It's even more important now because of how terrible I was then. When I asked you to marry me, you threw the fact that I didn't trust you back in my face. And I suppose I deserved it that way."

"Asked me? Demanded, you mean. You made it sound like a business proposition." She bit her lip as the feelings came flooding back. "It was insulting, Douglas," she added quietly.

He nodded. "You're right. I'm sorry. It was a rotten job I

made of that, all around." He leaned back and rubbed his neck. "It wasn't that I didn't trust you, *per se—*"

"Oh, really?" Taryn cut in sarcastically.

He looked at the ceiling and sighed, then bent to look at Chip as the dog whined softly. Rising quickly, he went to Chip, pulling up a footstool so he could face Taryn and stroke the dog at the same time. "In the wine cellar . . . that didn't work out as I'd hoped. I had a feeling something was going on between you and Todd, but I didn't know what. I watched Todd follow you with his eyes all day, and part of me began to realize that whatever was going on, you didn't have a willing part in it. I was scared for the inn, and scared for you. I knew he was the aggressor. But I couldn't get answers from him, or Carla, or you."

"I answered you. You didn't want to listen. You didn't want to believe me."

His lips tightened and he looked down at Chip. "I also got the feeling he was pursuing you, romantically. It ate at me. And ate and ate. Jealously is a hungry demon." He looked up at her then, gray eyes dark and intense. "When I came into the cellar and saw the two of you horsing around . . ."

"He was trying to threaten me, manipulate me. It wasn't horsing, believe me." She shuddered.

"You shut me out."

"We were all way too tense," she said as she shook her head. "Besides, you two would have come to blows. He'd have sued you, and the inn right out from under you."

Douglas turned his gaze back to Chip, who seemed to take comfort from his master's hand. "I never thought of that." He paused. "I was hurt, and angry, and terrified of losing everything that was important to me and not being able to do a damned thing about it. I felt the people in front of me had all the answers and wouldn't provide them. And then it all came together in my gut and I blurted out that proposal. I played my final card to keep you with me, but played it all wrong."

"I'm not going to argue with you there," she said with a wry smile.

"You were right. It did sound like a business proposal. I'll never do it again."

Her heart sank. She couldn't help it. Not that she'd been harboring hopes of another proposal—a woman couldn't expect a man to ask her more than once—but now that the words were out, she couldn't help feeling deflated. She reminded herself that she'd made the decision to come back to Aspen Creek regardless of how things went with Douglas. Seeing him on occasion would be enough, she told herself. She couldn't allow her expectations to run any higher than that.

"Look, let's back this up again." He rose and took her hands in his, pulling her to her feet. She let him, enjoying his strength and warmth, the way his hands completely enveloped hers. "I want to show you I trust you. I'm giving you the inn to prove it. I know you won't sell it off. I know you won't destroy it or run it into the ground. I trust you. Have we made it that far?" His eyes implored her.

Her thoughts were spinning. "I still can't accept the inn, just like that. That's just too extreme." She shook her head when he shrugged. "Douglas, it's crazy. And may I ask why this sudden change of heart? You didn't trust me then. Why now? I could argue that you trust me now simply because the danger has passed."

He grimaced. "That's fair enough. Tough, but fair. I can't say much in my defence."

She raised her brows. He squeezed her fingers in reply.

"Okay, I can't say anything in my defense. I'm after forgiveness now." He gave her a boyish grin that would cause any woman to forgive him just about anything. "Hence the deed for the inn, to try to make it up to you. You're not going to want my cabin too, are you?" He winked.

She couldn't help but laugh. "No. The inn is too much already."

"You need a home for your heart. The inn is it."

His words stopped the breath in her throat.

Headlights suddenly bobbed through the living room window, breaking the spell. "Tanley. The vet. Just when this was getting interesting." Douglas moved to rub his thumb gently along her lower lip. "We'll pick this up later."

Taryn sighed. It was just as well. She needed a few minutes to collect herself. After exchanging general chit-chat with the vet as they waited for Chip's sedative to take effect, Taryn took the opportunity to digest what Douglas had said. Something told her that her whole life was about to change yet again, and the effect was intoxicating. Or perhaps the man was intoxicating, she admitted, watching Douglas look on as the doctor put in the stitches and injected the antibiotics. Douglas raised his eyes to meet hers every few seconds, his intense gaze wreaking havoc on her concentration.

The ramifications of his words from the past few minutes were taking shape in her mind. *The rose. He'd missed her. Establishing trust.* He knew he was wrong in suspecting her and wanted her forgiveness. The loss of that burden alone made her feel strangely weightless, light-headed.

"He'll be fine," Dr. Tanley finally reported, rising to go. "He needs a few days of rest." He ran down a list of care instructions as he packed up his things, then Douglas saw him to his car.

Douglas returned and took Chip into the laundry area by the kitchen, talking softly to him as he put together a bed of blankets.

"Where were we?" he asked when he returned to Taryn's side.

"Trust."

"Ah, well, there's the thing. Guilty as I am, you can't exactly cast the first stone, can you? You didn't trust me either. I was rather insulted myself when I found out."

"What?" Why did she feel that she'd suddenly missed a large portion of their conversation?

"Carla." He saw her brows raise and smiled. "She called. I could hardly believe it."

"And what does that have to do with anything?"

"She called to let me know Todd was fired. You know about that? Good. She and Todd parted company, once she learned what he was about."

How much did she know? Did she blow the whistle on him?

"She was more concerned about him blackmailing you than the Staylander leak or the fact he was being hunted by his creditors. Said he deserved what he got. You didn't. You must have made a good impression on her. Not many women do, so count yourself lucky."

He shook his head then. "Holy cow, though, was she mad at him. She was never, ever that angry with me, and I hope she never is. The woman was spitting nails. Couldn't believe he'd throw gasoline onto his own professional funeral pyre." He frowned. "I think that's how she phrased it—by concocting a hair-brained scheme to blackmail you and try to foreclose on the inn." He nodded, almost to himself. "Anyway, she's afraid she might be seen as guilty, just by her association with him. Her professional reputation, you know," he added. "What I'd like to know is why you couldn't trust me with the fact that he was threatening you."

She sighed. "I didn't believe him. I was afraid to believe him, I guess. I refused to play. And since I knew I was innocent, I felt I could handle it on my own, if anything happened . . ."

When she let the silence drag, Douglas continued. "You should have told me, for professional reasons at the very least. I would have expected that from you. The situation could have severely affected the inn." His words became clipped. Reliving this was making him tense, that much was obvious. She could see it in his body language too, feel it in the stiffening of his arm on the back of the sofa behind her.

He was right. She was guilty of not trusting him, of being too proud. But, she realized now, she was a different person then. She'd changed. And for the better, she knew. Now, of course, if something like that happened, she'd go to him in an instant. Maybe there was no longer so much to prove.

Silence. He obviously wanted—and deserved—more. "You're right. I'm sorry," she finally said. "I should have told you." She turned to him, her eyes searching his face for understanding. She saw his lips curve ever so slightly, and knew she'd found the understanding she'd sought. "I would now." She added, smiling shyly.

Douglas appeared calmer now that it was out, taking her hand again, stroking the tops of her fingers with his thumb. When she didn't say more he went on. "He's out of the way now. You don't need to worry about him anymore."

"What do you mean?"

He seemed surprised that this was news to her, pulling his head back to look at her. "He's left the country. Didn't you know that?"

She was shocked. "No. For good?"

He smiled, almost smugly. "For a long time. If he comes back, he'll likely be arrested."

"Arrested for what?"

"Tax evasion, for one thing. I threatened to have him audited. Likely fraud too, after the audit. We accountants aren't completely without ammunition, you know. A number of my old classmates work for the government's taxation center. Why do you think he didn't follow through on his threat to drag your name through the mud when the Staylander leak was uncovered?"

"How?" Taryn managed to say, while staring at him in surprise.

"I started looking into his personal finances the moment I found out about his take-over plans. It took until last week to get all the details sorted out so I could make my phone call to him."

She stopped breathing for a moment. "Thank you," she whispered, suddenly feeling very free, and very protected.

They sat quietly for a minute or so. She tried to put all the pieces of their conversation together. She felt so relaxed now, as if her body were sinking lower into the sofa, although she knew she hadn't moved at all. She sighed deeply, her head pressed against the cushioned backrest. His hand came to her hair. She felt him pluck at a curl, pulling it and letting it spring back. She smiled. His touch was glorious, she didn't want to move, ever again.

"But . . ." She dragged her concentration back to the matter at hand. "Can we get back to this business with the inn? Why do you feel you need to *give* me the inn to prove your trust? Why not just hire me back?"

"I didn't know if that'd be a big enough draw. You'd come back?"

In a heartbeat. She nodded her assent.

"And here I was ready to move to Vancouver to court you properly."

She had noticed the luggage was more than what was needed for a business trip. "Move?"

"For a while. For as long as it took."

It would have been a considerable sacrifice on his part. She knew how much living here meant to him. "I'm very flattered."

"Flattered. Hmmmm." He leaned closer, lowering his voice. "I was hoping for 'swept off your feet,' but then again, I'm just getting started."

Taryn felt his finger trace the edge of her ear, light as a feather, and marveled again at how such a large, strong, rugged man could possess such a soft touch. A small hum of laughter vibrated deep in her throat, brought on by the tickling sensation or simple giddiness—she wasn't sure and didn't care. The man was an incorrigible and wonderfully effective flirt. While she let herself enjoy his touch, she gathered enough common sense to almost absently remind him, "Regardless, I can't take the inn."

"A home for your heart, remember?"

Only if you came with it. "That's a beautiful thought," she whispered. "But it belongs to your family and should stay in your family."

"We'll see what we can do about that then."

She cocked her head. "You're full of odd quips this evening, aren't you?"

He leaned back and looked at the ceiling, running both hands through his hair. "Hell, I'm blowing this one too." He suddenly rose from the sofa, pulling her up with him. "Come with me. I'm going to do this right."

"Where—"

He spun her gracefully around in what felt like a formal ballroom dance step. She found herself pressed against his body, her arm pulled around her own waist, his arm around her. With his free hand he put a finger to her lips. She smiled under it. "Do you trust me?"

She nodded. *With my life. With my heart.*

"And I trust you. You know that now? You forgive me for before?"

She smiled and nodded. The past no longer mattered, no longer hurt. "But you don't have to prove it by giving me—"

He pressed his finger to her lips again. "That's all we need to know, for now. Don't move." He strode over to the charcoal suit hanging by the entrance. She heard him rustling the protective travel plastic. He returned and took her hand. "Come outside." He led her through the kitchen, pausing, without letting go of her hand, to check on Chip, who was sleeping soundly. He unlocked the French doors, swinging them open to the back porch. It was a wide, planked expanse with natural log railings. Just below them, the land dropped away sharply, giving the impression that the cabin floated on the edge of the treed valley before them.

The night air felt cold, heavy, and still on her skin.

Moonlight painted the pine treetops with a magical silver brush, and millions of individual pine needles glistened with a light frost, catching the moon's cool, pale glow. Taryn's gaze followed the view to the horizon, where Venus hung low and bright, an age-old beacon for lovers. Her eyes were then drawn upward, to the star-scattered sky. She could never, ever tire of a view like this.

"Listen," he said. She did, and heard the distant rush of water.

"The falls," she said.

"Yes. The falls. Remember our time there? It wasn't so long ago." He pulled her gently before him so that her back pressed against his chest, and held her hands with his in front of her.

She nodded. The crisp night air chilled her skin and she burrowed contentedly against his warm body, no longer shy about enjoying his warmth.

"When I kissed you there, that day . . . It was all I could do to stop." His breath warmed her ear. "But I'd given you my word." He turned her toward him. She sensed the intensity of his gaze in the darkness, his heat, his strength, and suddenly felt soft, feminine, and willingly pliant. "I want to make it right, Taryn. I want us to do things right. By the rules. And then I don't ever want to stop again."

His lips claimed hers with confident intimacy, warm and secure, and at the same time exciting, promising a union that would break barriers and ignore inhibitions. Her skin buzzed. She sagged against him as her bones seemed to fill with sand.

He held her, tight, strong, able, then pulled back to retrieve something from his shirt pocket. Without taking his eyes from hers, he pressed it into her hand.

"What—" She began to look down.

He stopped her words with another quick kiss, then moved his head back just far enough away to speak, his gaze intently holding hers. "Taryn Christiansen," he whispered, "would you please do me the honor of becoming my wife?"

Taryn jerked her head back with a sharp intake of breath, searching his face. "But you just said you'd never propose again," she blurted out, belatedly realizing the stupidity of the comment. *What on earth did it matter what he said a few minutes ago! Answer the question!* She'd thought this was all leading up to the beginning of a dating relationship, and that assumption alone was enough to send her heart soaring. But this! It was more than she'd hoped for!

His brow folded in thought. His lips fought a perplexed smile. "Hmmm. Not quite the response I was expecting. When did I say that? Oh . . . no," he said as realization obviously hit him. "I meant I'd never do it that poorly again. You know, an unromantic business proposition." He held her face in his hands. "This is better, isn't it?"

"Much," she agreed, relaxing again.

"And? How about third time lucky? I love you, Taryn. Will you marry me?" He brought her hand holding the small box up between them and flipped the lid, revealing a ring with an exquisitely simple solitaire diamond. "I bought this the day after you left, determined that you'd wear it one day. I wasn't giving up on us. Ever."

The diamond caught a sparkle of light from the moon, as if winking at her. She closed her hand over it. "I love you too, Douglas Prescott. And yes, I'll marry you," she whispered, then kissed him soundly, and with all of her heart.